RYANN FLETCHER

Polar Opposites

Cover art by Sarah Holmes @ANebulousPurpose

First edition

ISBN: 978-1-7399953-8-6

This book was professionally typeset on Reedsy.
Find out more at reedsy.com

For everyone discovering who they really are

Contents

Chapter 1

Snow sparkled against the distant, sloped peak, the mid-morning sun reflecting off the mountain and down onto the road that approached the lodge. Max flipped down the visor, flinching from the receipt she forgot she'd stashed up there at the last stop for gas, an expensive tank she'd had to put on her credit card. One more mile to the lodge and she could collapse into her cabin. There was a time she could have done a six hour drive with no problem, but that was before she'd found herself alone in the front seat.

Static hissed from the radio, and she twisted the knob to turn it off. The lodge was too far from a radio tower, and the land was too hilly up here to get any kind of decent signal. She'd be living off whatever music she'd remembered to pile onto her phone until the end of the winter break season, and in that exact moment, she remembered that she'd forgotten to transfer the files. They were organized neatly by artist and genre, in folders sitting untouched on the desktop of her computer, a few hundred miles to the south.

Max groaned, lightly smacking the steering wheel as she pulled into the lodge's driveway. It was the same as it had been the previous year, and the year before that, as long as she'd been going to Crimson Oak. She parked, climbing out of the driver's seat and slamming the lightly rusted door behind her. Checking her reflection in the side mirror, she bent to examine a stray lock of short, dark hair springing from the back. She frowned and pressed it down, ruffling her pixie cut in the process.

It was unusually warm for the start of the season, with no snow except at the peak of Bear Mountain. Her lined boots were heavy and hot, and she was regretting not packing something else.

"Checking in," she said, pushing through the door of reception. Bells tied to the top jingled lightly as she stepped over the threshold, blinking into the relative darkness. "Max Carter, instructor."

"Max!" Orren yelled. "You're back!"

Her eyes adjusted, and she smiled, leaning against the desk. He looked the same as he always had, his dark skin unblemished, unwrinkled, despite the fact he easily had twenty years on her. Max grinned at him, flashing a smile. "It's me, in the flesh."

"Nice to see you again. Same as last year?"

"Unless Mr. Parker found it in his heart to give us all a nice big raise."

Orren rolled his eyes. "Yeah, as if there's any chance of that happening. I'm surprised any of us are even here this year, with this weather we've been having."

"Yeah, it's a little warm, Orr. Where are you keeping all the snow?"

"My back pocket, obviously." He slid a stack of forms across the desk, secured by three silver paper clips. "The usual."

"Yeah, yeah." Max signed each form, one after another, with her tiny, cramped scrawl of a signature, barely legible but definitely unique. "Anyone else arrive yet?"

"It's just you this year, Max."

She put the pen down. "What?"

Orren shrugged. "Snowboarding program got cut, didn't they tell you? Mr. Parker is on the ropes with this place, some big conglomerate wants to buy the lodge. He's probably going to take the bait, but he wants to juice profits first. It will get a better price that way."

"Oh." Max swallowed hard, the realization sinking into her gut like a stone. "So this is probably the last year for all of us, then."

"He said the new owners agreed to keep on as much staff as they could."

"We all know what that means." Max sighed, picking up the pen to sign the remaining forms. "What about ski instructors, then?"

"They're flying in some hotshot from the Rockies. She almost went national, I hear."

"So only two instructors, one for ski, one for snowboarding?"

"That's not all," Orren said apologetically. "Mr. Parker said whichever program performs worse gets the boot mid-season."

Max smacked her palm against the desk. "What? Why?"

"Same reason. Less staffing costs means bigger profits, and there haven't exactly been tons of people booking trips, not with the weather being what it is. Mr. Parker—"

"Mr. Parker wants to get as big a payout he can, and to hell with the rest of us," Max snarled. "If I had known before I drove up, I wouldn't have even bothered."

"That's a lie, and we both know it," Orren said lightly, taking the signed forms back and straightening them. "You couldn't stay off this mountain if your life depended on it."

"So what kind of occupancy are we looking at, here? Half?"

"A quarter."

Max gave a low whistle, leaning forward against the desk. "Ouch."

"Might get better by next week, you know the start of December is always more of a jumpstart for the season. It's early, yet, for here."

"We'd better hope so, or he'll have this lodge functioning as a ghost town until the sale is done."

The door's bells jingled once more, and Max turned, an eyebrow raised at the perfectly coiffed, perfectly matching, perfectly composed skier, who looked like she'd stepped right out of Winter Sports magazine. She flipped her shoulder-length hair over her shoulder as though she was already in a photo shoot.

"Sloane Hearst, checking in."

"Ah, Ms. Hearst," Orren said, flipping through a stack of papers. "You're our new ski instructor."

"This mountain isn't very impressive, is it?" Sloane said, arms folded over her chest. "I've seen bunny slopes with a steeper grade."

Max laughed. "Trust me, the trails up there are more of a challenge than they first seem. Lots of little jumps, obstacles, and there's the ski jump on the other side." She held out her hand. "Max Carter. I'm the snowboard instructor."

"I didn't know they offered snowboarding here."

Max pulled her hand back. She recognized that tone, that lightly dismissive way of addressing her. Damned skiers. "They have for a number of years now. I'm sorry that your cursory internet search failed to tell you that."

"Given I was pulled in at the last minute to boost the lodge's attendance, I didn't have much time to scope things out." Sloane removed her thin gloves, stashing them in her pockets. "Clearly their snowboard instructor wasn't quite pulling in the numbers."

"I'll have you know that I grew this program from nothing," Max snapped. "Who even are you, Sloane Hearst? Some up-jumped ski fanatic who almost went national, but couldn't quite hack it? Wow, what a legacy, to almost have been someone important."

Orren cleared his throat. "Alright, then," he said, sliding a stack of papers to Sloane. "Max, it's the same as last year, if you want to go settle in." Max opened her mouth to let another snide remark loose, but he shot her a warning look, and she put her hands up in surrender.

"Whatever. You know where to find me if you need me. When's first lesson?"

"You're booked in for ten tomorrow morning." He slid a thick folder across the desk. "Your lanyard and tags are all in here, should be everything you need, I'd imagine. You've been here long enough, you know the ropes."

"What's the deal with food this year?"

"Same as last year, you can pick up leftovers from the back of the kitchen. Reduced staff this year, though, so—"

Max rolled her eyes. "Yeah. Of course."

"Linens are in bags by the door," Orren said with a nod. "Same as always, you can get the laundry machines for two hours on Sundays between changeovers."

"Roger that," she replied, hefting the canvas bag over her shoulder. "Did they ever get that messed up washing machine fixed from last year? Wringing out my clothes by hand got real old after a couple of weeks."

Orren grimaced apologetically, waving an arm at her. "You know how it is." He tugged at his plaid jacket, adjusting the zipper that ran from one shoulder to the opposite hip. "If you get there early, you'll be able to grab the good machine. Might be easier this year with less staff?"

"Silver linings," Max replied with another eye roll. She shot a look at the ski instructor and her rigid posture before she opened the door. "I'll come by in the morning for my schedule, Orren."

He waved at her, and she adjusted the weight of the canvas bag, distributing it over her shoulder. Gravel crunched under her boots as she walked back to her small utility vehicle, frowning at the amount of mud caked along the underside. It was too wet for late November. Too much rain, not enough snow, and the mountain would be even more treacherous than it usually was.

That ski instructor would learn soon enough that Bear Mountain wasn't as tame as it appeared. Max checked the calendar on her phone. The full moon was in three days, and she was already yearning for the icy air of the summit.

* * *

The cabin was just as she remembered it, the only difference being the fine coating of dust across every surface. Max coughed as she brushed it from the desk, the wardrobe, the chest of drawers, almost enjoying the sparkle of it in the afternoon light as it drifted through the air, still circulating from when she'd opened the door.

She dropped her bags on the floor, stretching her arms up over her head. Six weeks of good boarding would clear her head, would let her feel like she had some sort of grip on her life again. Winter was like rain after a drought for her, like opening up as a lotus flower after months of clinging to the edge of being able to keep on getting out of bed every day. The crisp, frigid temperatures were a balm against the burn of existence, ever present, ever pressing down, ever constant.

She was almost thirty, and what did she have to show for it? A seasonal job at a winter sports lodge? A shared apartment with four roommates she could barely stand? Weekends filled with last minute shifts at the diner, a town she was desperate to leave behind forever, a stream of failed relationships a mile long, and parents she hadn't spoken to in almost a year. Some people didn't deserve to have space in her life, not after nearly three decades of snide remarks, undermining, demanding.

Max pulled sheets from the linen bag, spreading them over the bottom bunk. She tucked each edge around the mattress, smoothing the wrinkles from the faded, brushed fleece, soft beneath her fingertips, and bleached whiter than the snow at the peak of the mountain. That snow was still tinged with green, the persistent grass growing up and through until it got cold enough. It should have been cold enough weeks prior, but with the way things were going, snowboarding season was only going to get shorter and shorter.

Fitted sheet, top sheet, comforter. She hung the towels on the hooks in the bathroom, wiping months of disuse from the mirror. Max leaned her forehead against the glass, her short dark hair reflecting back at her. One last season at the Crimson Oak Lodge, and then it would wind up gutted and reformed into another corporate retreat spot for companies trying to force their employees into friendship with team building and breakout sessions. She'd rather be on the slopes, and in fact, she was going to do just that before the sun went down.

Shrugging her parka back on over her shoulders, she zipped it, ignoring the frayed threads at the cuffs. The door slammed shut behind her, and she unhooked her board from the rack on top of her car, parked outside her cabin. It was covered in splashes of neon, the wolf on the underside perfectly waxed. She was glad she'd done it before coming up, because the last thing she wanted to be was trapped in her cabin, methodically spreading wax over the fissures and cracks in the barrier.

The mountain called to her, the same way it had when she'd first seen it, aged thirteen. She'd been on a school trip, then, and fallen on her face more times than she could count, but as soon as she was able to work, she did, coming back at least once every season to feel the wind on her face and watch the sun set over distant hills, buried down beneath what was left of the changing leaves.

Most branches that time of year, nearly December, should have been bare, but at least a third still held their foliage, and it blazed in the orange hue of the setting sun. If Mr. Parker was a smart man, and clearly he was not, he'd be using Crimson Oak Lodge year round, but he didn't want to pay the staffing costs.

Max waited for the next chair on the lift, sliding into it like a favorite pair of jeans when it arrived. It carried her up the slope, and she looked out over the mountain, breathing deep the almost sickly thick scent of pine. Six weeks of freedom, and then a return to the crushing normality. She'd stay on Bear Mountain forever if she could, running through the trees, staring up at the unimpeded sky stricken with stars, and not having to pick the remains of someone else's breakfast out of the sink strainer. Living alone felt like an impossible dream, but for six weeks, she'd have her own space.

She exhaled slowly, letting the pressures and stress roll off of her in waves, more and more the closer she got to the peak. Clouds drifted lazily in the distance, wispy and hazy, certainly not heavy with snow like they should be, but as she leaped from the chair onto the mountain, she felt like she was home.

Snapping her boots onto her board, Max squared her shoulders, ready to remember the feeling of flying. Being alone on the mountain was the key to everything, the only thing she thought about the other 10 months of the year. She'd always wished that the lodge would be open through more of the season, but with the changing weather, that was becoming less and less likely.

She started down the mountain, focusing on the feelings of gravity and friction and the distant, edging prickle beneath her skin that had already begun, days before the full moon. She didn't mind what she was, but had to conceal it on the mountain. It was why she doused herself in enough scent neutralizers to cover an entire pack, and why she only stayed six weeks. If anyone was going to get suspicious that she got sick every full moon, it would be Orren. The man never missed anything.

The snow was warm and slushy beneath her board, putting drag on her speed. It wasn't terrible for a first ride of the season, and she jumped a small ramp with ease, landing perfectly as she went. With every weave between posts, every slide, every tree that she passed, she remembered how to breathe a little easier.

Chapter 2

Sloane clipped into her skis, paused at the top of the mountain. She frowned at the piste, snow already carved out of the shallower sections. Clearly, she wasn't the first one on the slopes. She tugged her goggles down over her eyes, trying not to stare into the sunset, despite its beauty.

The wet slush was almost sticky beneath her skis, and it would only be a moderate speed to the bottom, a disappointment. One more in a long string of recent failures, all of them stacked up neatly against her name, an embarrassment, another failed athlete, another reason that she was ready to give it all up, never look at another pair of skis in her life, move somewhere hot that was never so much as touched by snow.

She wove in and out of the tree line, avoiding the abrasions clearly caused by a snowboard. The lodge she used to teach at didn't allow snowboarders because of the damage they did to the piste, but the lodge she used to teach at had unceremoniously cut her loose when she failed to make the nationals team. A quiet word in the manager's office, and that was that. No notice, no apologies, not even an offer of a decent reference as she was sent packing with no other plan for the winter season.

It was too late to get a job somewhere else, many other resorts had already started their seasons, and going home felt like an admission of failure, one she'd have to make eventually, but wasn't quite ready to. Maybe she wouldn't ever be ready. Maybe she could stay on this crappy little mountain for the rest of her life, and no one would ever ask where she'd gone.

Going from the cover of Winter Sports Magazine to relegated to a short-season lodge in the middle of the midwest was a long way to fall, and it had happened so fast. She'd been the darling of nationals predictions, a shoo-in, a sure choice, and then... well. And then qualifiers had been over last month's full moon, a last-minute reschedule to make space in the roster for the snowboarders, newly added to the nationals competition.

She bent, trying to pick up as much speed as she could on the wet slopes. Maybe if she was fast enough, she could outrun her own thoughts. Pine trees at the edges of the run glittered in the setting sun, the branches dripping with melting snow. Sloane grunted softly to herself, weaving side to side, in between flagged poles and out again, wondering what might have been if she wasn't what she was.

She'd been what she was for two decades, a proud family tradition, a natural advantage on the slopes at times, a deeper connection with mountain and earth and cold that always led her back to careening down the piste because at least then, no one could chastise her in the moment.

No, the chastisement always came later.

Sometimes, she wished that she'd never stepped into skis in the first place. Decades of pressure had stripped away all the exhilaration and joy of it, leaving her with a strange sense of obligation and inescapability from something she'd spent too long to be good at to just give up. Where did you go, when suddenly all the doors were closing? When you'd spent years working up to a standard that was no longer needed, and you'd never bothered to nurture anything else?

Her ski hit a rut and she nearly stumbled, recovering just in time to reach the bottom and finding the other instructor there. "You carved up the piste," Sloane said, coming to a stop.

"Snow is bad, you'd have done the same if you'd been first."

"I doubt that."

Max snorted. "Why am I not surprised that you're one of those skiers who thinks you should have the slopes all to yourself?"

"It's about conservation."

"It's about more than that and you know it. Let me guess, wherever you used to work didn't allow boards?"

"No," Sloane answered, her mouth set into a frown. "They did not."

"Maybe you should go back there, then, if it was so much better than here."

"It's too late in the season. I'm here, now, and besides, I didn't sit on a plane for four hours just to turn around after one ride down the slope."

"Oh no, four hours on a plane, what a hardship." Max laughed again, pulling off the knitted hat she was wearing, sending a spray of snow to the ground. "I drove here, it took six hours."

"It's not a competition."

"Isn't it?"

Sloane narrowed her eyes. "What is that supposed to mean?" She looked to the tree line, wishing she could escape, wishing it was already the full moon, wishing she could lay on the forest floor and let it claim her.

"I guess Orren didn't fill you in, seeing as you're a newbie. We're the only two instructors, princess."

"I knew that."

"And whoever gets fewer students gets the boot mid-season."

"Oh." Sloane smiled. "I'm not worried about that. Skiing tends to be more popular."

Max raised an eyebrow. "Maybe where you're from. I wouldn't write me off that quickly." She twisted on her board, looking back to the tow-line. "Boarding was added to nationals, I'm sure you heard. We're here to stay."

"Well then, Max Carter, I look forward to the challenge. But you should know, I've never lost a bet." A lie, but convincingly delivered. Sloane had developed that skill long ago. "May the best instructor win."

"I plan to."

"What makes you so sure that you're the best?"

"I've been on this mountain for years, I know every nook and cranny of it," Max answered, still looking out over the mountain. "I have loyal students, and I'm good at what I do." She glanced back at Sloane, a smirk playing at her full lips. "Besides, you Rockies types always think you know everything, but you don't. The snow here is different."

"Snow is snow."

"Yet you followed me down the piste just to tell me I'd carved it out, when I clearly didn't. Snow is snow? Please."

Sloane leaned on one of her poles, tugging her goggles down to hang around her neck, light beginning to fade over parts of the mountain. "You might think you know everything there is to know just because you're from around here—"

"I'm not from around here."

"But I've spent most of my life on the slopes, and I known damned well what it looks like when a board has carved slices into the snow."

Max threw her head back, laughing. "Get your eyes checked."

"My vision is twenty-twenty, thank you, and I'd think someone with so much experience would be capable of boarding down without leaving a path of destruction in your wake." Sloane gestured behind her at the mountain. "If we have to share these slopes, then I'm going to ask you to maintain at least a semblance of courtesy."

"What is your problem?"

"Excuse me?"

"Ever since you stumbled your way into reception, you've had an attitude with me. Why is that? Is it that I snowboard, or is it that I'm not part of your posh little circles?"

"*Excuse me?*" Sloane repeated. "You don't know the first thing about me."

"I know that you showed up here with brand new gear that's easily as much as I make in a month back home. I also know that you clearly have a problem with snowboarders, which doesn't surprise me."

Their breath clouded in front of them with the dropping temperature that the night always brought. Sloane cleared her throat and straightened her posture, raising an eyebrow. "I was almost on the national team. My gear was paid for by sponsors."

"*Almost* on nationals."

Sloane's stomach burned, and heat crept up her neck. "I think it's best if we just stay out of each other's way for the duration of this."

"You're more than welcome to step down if you can't handle the slopes."

"I'm not going anywhere." She pulled her goggles back over her eyes, easing forward towards the ski-tow. "Well, I mean, I am *now*, but not from the lodge. I just don't want to talk to you anymore." Sloane cringed at herself, and hoped the growing darkness hid it. "Good night."

"Sure thing, princess," Max replied, laughing. "We'll see how long you last."

"I'll last longer than you!" Again, she wanted the mountain to swallow her. "Stop carving up my mountain!"

"*Your* mountain?"

"Yes, *my* mountain, when everything is said and done." Sloane was still shouting over her shoulder as she approached the lift. "Don't underestimate me."

"I don't even think that's possible," Max called. "I couldn't estimate you any lower than I already do."

Sloane bent her knees as the chair came up behind her legs, pulling the bar down over herself. Her jaw pulsed, tensing over and over, persisting past the point where a headache began to match the rhythm pounding in her ears. She never should have come to Crimson Oak, it was a mistake. She should have just laid low for the season and tried again next year, if they'd still have her. Probably not, now that they had a full team.

An opportunity lost, a dream, withered on the vine. It was the end of the only thing she'd ever dreamed of, and instead of nursing her wounds, she was busy trying to prove a point. Halfway across the country, at a small, mid-range lodge, in direct competition with another instructor, and nothing could ever feel worse. She longed for the safety of her old apartment, but that was long gone. It was only for athletes training for nationals. Now, she was no one at all.

Just one more burnout.

She hissed quietly to herself, chiding herself for being so absorbed in her own misery. The best thing to do was to get back on the slopes, get back to doing what she knew she was good at, nationals or no, and to forget about the whole thing for a while. Six weeks would be long enough for most of the sports press to disappear, and the peace she'd get after was worth running off to hide at Crimson Oak Lodge.

Sloane exited the lift, unclipping her boots from her skis with the back of her pole. She picked up her skis, heading back to her cabin for a hot shower and a soft bed. At least she had her own space, if she had to share with that other instructor, they'd probably kill each other. At least *that* would save on staffing costs.

The sun was almost completely buried in the growing night sky by then, the first stars beginning to prick through the thick, hazy blanket of blue. The darkness came fast in winter, but out there, beyond the mountain, was just darkness. The nearest decent sized town was almost twenty miles north, and she'd passed through it on her way up. It was a level of rural resignation she wasn't used to, and the absence of lights in the distance almost spooked her, pricking the hairs at the back of her neck.

Of course, in a few nights, she'd be the scariest thing on the mountain. There was a strange freedom in what she was, the innate need to ignore everything else pressing for a night. There was no stopping it, once it started, and she'd grown to enjoy the crisp, frozen abandonment of hunting in the dead of night. Bear Mountain would make a nice place to explore, assuming no one got in her way. Low visitor numbers were good for something at least, she supposed.

Pushing open the cabin door, she kicked the remaining snow from her boots, slipping out of them and tugging up her insulated socks. She closed the door, hanging her pristine white coat on a wall hook with a heavy sigh.

At least she had time to catch up on the book she'd started reading twelve times and abandoned each time, sliding it back into her bag, unread.

Chapter 3

Max had awoken early enough to catch a morning session on the slopes, allowing the crisp scent of pine to cleanse her, to remind her who she was and what she wanted, and after an hour, it settled deep in her bones, the thought that all she'd ever wanted was to spend her life on that mountain. There was nothing more than the sound of her board against the slushy snow, the gentle breeze through the needles of the conifers, and her own steady, measured breaths.

The ski-tow pulled her back to the top once more, but this time, she unstrapped from her board, picking it up to carry under her arm. Pushing the door to reception open, she yawned, ready for coffee. "Morning, Orren," she said, leaning the board against the wood-paneled wall.

"Ms. Carter," he replied, nodding to her. "They say snow is forecast for tomorrow, we could be full up by the end of the week."

Max bent, looking out the window, and frowned at the cloudless sky. "I don't know about that one."

"Are you an amateur meteorologist now?"

"No, I just know this mountain, and there's no snow up there." She turned back towards the desk, heading for the coffee station. "Not yet, anyway."

"You know the kitchen will give you coffee if you ask."

"Yes, but then I'd miss out on talking to you, and that's the highlight of my mornings here, Mr. Ralt."

Orren rolled his eyes, but smiled. "We did get a couple of people in for a long weekend stay last night. Maybe if you work your magic, you can talk one of them into some lessons."

"Who have we got?"

"An Amber Pennington, she's new this year, and someone named Chad Carrington. He's never been to Crimson Oak before, but he looks experienced. Rude man, if you ask me."

"Anyone with a name like Chad Willoughsby is bound to be rude. Give him to Sloane, I'm sure they'd get along perfectly. Birds of a feather and all that."

"Mm." Orren raised an eyebrow at her. "Is she getting under your skin?"

"You could say that." Max stirred powdered creamer into her coffee, adding two spoons of sugar. "She tried to corner me on the slope last night, accusing me of carving up *her* mountain."

"I can only imagine how well that didn't go."

"People like her are entitled. She walks around thinking she owns everything, you know? It's obnoxious. I've been working every season here for twelve years, she shows up looking like she stepped out of a damned catalog and I'm supposed to, what, roll over and play dead?"

"I'm a neutral party here," Orren said, holding his hands up in surrender. "I don't want to find myself in the crossfire."

"Crossfire," Max repeated with a scoff. "She'll be lucky if she even gets a shot off."

"Don't underestimate Sloane Hearst, that's all I'll say."

"Why, is she going to sue me to death? She looks like the kind that has a penchant for unnecessary litigation. I bet I could take her in a fair fight."

"Max—"

"I'm not going to actually fight her, Orren, relax." Max stirred the coffee before taking a careful sip. "Even as much as I may want to."

"She's a skilled skier."

"Whose side are you on, anyway?"

Orren sighed, straightening a pile of papers on his desk. "I'm not on anyone's side. I just don't want to see this place fall apart."

"Any news on the sale?"

"Not yet, although I imagine it won't be too long before we do. A few weeks, maybe. Before Christmas, if I had to guess." He leaned back in his chair, swiveling gently from side to side before continuing. "How much are you going to want to kill me where I sit if I tell you that it's up to remaining staff to get this place decorated for the holidays?"

"That depends on whether it was your idea or not."

He rolled his eyes. "Of course it wasn't my idea. You think my idea of a fun time is stapling tangled strings of lights to the banisters?"

"What's the deadline on that?"

"End of the week. Although, given the... rather frustrating lack of guests, and by that measure, lack of clients for you, I'm sure it won't be too challenging to achieve, time-wise."

Max swallowed a gulp of coffee, savoring the familiar bitter taste as it ran down her throat. "Have you asked the princess yet?"

"No, not yet. I will when I see her."

"Looks like the early bird gets the extra chores, then."

"She'll get her fair share, don't you worry." Orren stood, giving the empty coffee pot a stern glance. "You could at least refill it if you're the last one."

"You didn't even give me a chance!" Max protested, laughing. She took the pot from the stand, waving him off as she pulled open the door to the back room. "You're worse than my mother, Orren."

"Well, *someone* has to make sure you don't get completely feral up here, don't they? If I wasn't here keeping the roof on this place, we both know you'd be running rampant all over the slopes, probably getting yourself into all kinds of trouble."

Max stood over the small sink, filling the pot with water. "Only the good kind of trouble," she called over her shoulder through the door. "You know me, I can't resist—" She was interrupted by the delicate jingle of the bells on the door, and she stopped, waiting in the back room.

"Ms. Pennington," Orren announced, his voice muted through the door. "How can I help you?"

"I was told when I booked over the phone that there would be instructors at this lodge, but I just stood at the top of the piste for twenty minutes, and no one came to assist me."

"I apologize, ma'am, we didn't have you booked in for any lessons. Whom did you speak to, when making your booking?"

"Surely when your resort is this empty, your instructors should be clamoring for work. I didn't book a slot, because given all the empty rooms in the hotel, I didn't assume it would be busy."

Orren cleared his throat. "Ma'am, I'm very sorry, I will get someone for you as soon as possible. What kind of instruction are you hoping for?"

Max pushed through the door, setting the coffee pot full of water on Orren's desk. She held out her hand with a broad, winning smile, taking in the woman's perfectly curled hair, draped over her brand new parka and matching ski pants. "Good morning, ma'am, my name is Max Carter, I'm a snowboard instructor here at Crimson Oak."

"Snowboard," the woman said carefully. "I've never tried that."

"It's never too late to try, right, Ms. Pennington?"

The woman cocked an eyebrow and smiled. "You can call me Amber."

"An absolute pleasure to meet you. If you don't have a board, I have some spares up at the ski-tow, inside the operator's booth, along with some other gear."

"Wonderful. I just love a morning on the slopes, don't you?"

Max smiled at her. "I live for it."

"Well, let's get started then, shall we?" Amber threw open the door to the outside, heading straight for the ski-tow.

"I've got this, Orren," Max said, just loud enough for him to hear. "Don't worry."

"I'm only worried about you when you're getting into trouble," he shot back in a stage whisper.

"I dunno, she looks like she might be into trouble, don't you think?" Max winked at him, laughing at his horrified face. "Don't worry, I won't do anything to get myself fired." She smirked. "Probably."

Amber was already waiting at the tow line, a hand on her hip. She was beautiful in the way that roses were. Stunning, perfectly kept, but would ruin your life if you got too close. Her chic grey goggles hung around her neck, glinting gently in the morning sunlight.

"Ms. Pennington—Amber," Max corrected herself. "So, how long have you been coming to Crimson Oak?"

"First time here this year. I had some... rather unfortunate circumstances this time last year, and with my kids away at school, I needed a distraction."

"I'm sorry to hear about the unfortunate circumstances." Max knocked on the control door. "It's Carter, I need boarding gear for a client."

The door opened, and a bored-looking teenager peered out. "Take whatever you want, I'm not paid enough to care."

"First year working?" Max asked.

"Yeah." She looked down at her phone again, plugged into a portable battery. "Better than working as an elf at the mall, at least."

Max laughed, choosing a board and boots for Amber. "I think almost anything is better than working as an elf at the mall." She nodded, preparing to close the door. "Thanks."

"Whatever."

"Alright, Amber, I've got some gear here for your first snowboarding lesson. Are you excited?" Max asked. "I remember my first lesson, I was thirteen, and it was right here in this spot."

"You've been here a long time, then," Amber replied. "Are you a townie?"

"Uh—no, I'm not. I live a few hours south of here. I drive up every season."

"What do you do the rest of the year?"

Max turned, bending to lay the board on the ground. "Oh, you know, this and that. I live for the slopes, though."

"Sometimes I wish I was more like you, someone who had a deep passion for something other than themselves. It's a wonder to experience that kind of exhilaration, don't you think?"

"Sure," Max replied, gesturing for her to step into the snowboarding boots. "I guess I'm a bit of a loner the rest of the year. I don't get out too much."

"Amber?" Sloane called as she skied in from the cabins on impressively intact skis. "I haven't seen you in forever! How are you?"

"Sloane! When I saw you last, you were still in college. You've certainly grown up, haven't you?"

Sloane laughed, an irritatingly light and manufactured tinkle. "Even I can't escape the passage of time." She frowned at Max. "What brings you to Crimson Oak, Amber?"

"I just needed to get away, you know? Life feels too heavy, it's oppressive. Sometimes you just have to take the world by the horns and do something for yourself. The house is empty, I'm at a loose end, it just made sense."

"And you're... taking snowboard lessons?"

"If I'd have known you were here, I would have waited, of course."

Max ground her teeth together, trying to resist the urge to launch Sloane off the side of the mountain. "Amber, we can get started as soon as you're ready."

Ignoring her, Amber continued. "What was all that nasty business with nationals, then? I heard some dreadful things through the grapevine."

Sloane jerked away from the comment, leaning back on her ski poles. "Oh? And what was that you heard, then?"

"That you were disqualified. Performance enhancers, Sloane, really?"

"I didn't—that's not—"

"There's no need for all that with me, darling, we all know everyone does it, even the amateurs with something to prove. Honestly, I'd have been surprised if you *weren't* partaking in enhancers, given how good you were doing."

"It wasn't that, but thank you for your concern." Sloane's expression faltered, cycling through a wan smile, frustration, and settling back into her dazzling upper-crust demeanor. "So, Amber. Snowboarding?" She scrunched up her face. "In second-hand boots?"

Max swallowed back a growl. "It's perfectly fine to—"

"Oh you know, I told her that I'd rather not, but she all but twisted my arm, didn't you, Ms. Carter?"

"I don't quite recall it that way," Max said through gritted teeth.

"I've always preferred skiing, it's just so much more... civilized, don't you think, Sloane?"

"Of course, ma'am. It's why I prefer to ski where boards are prohibited, but it's becoming rarer and rarer these days. Seems like everyone is desperate to participate in the death of a time-honored winter sport." Sloane turned and smiled at Max, flashing too many teeth for it to be genuine. "I think I can take it from here."

Heat crawled up the side of Max's face, and her muscles gripped too hard against gravity, pulling prickles to rise up just beneath the skin. She breathed in a shaky breath, straightening. The full moon was only one more day away, and if she wasn't careful, she'd lose control. "Sure thing."

Sloane waved her away, and as Max opened the control door again, she hissed out a sigh, the force of it almost whistling as it crossed her lips. "Thanks again," she said, dumping the gear back in its box. Wordlessly, she marched back to reception, nearly tearing the door from its hinges.

"Whoa," Orren said, jumping up from his chair. "What the hell happened to you?"

"Sloane Hearst is the *worst* person I have ever met in my life, and I work retail nine months of the year." Max flexed her fingers into fists at her sides, releasing, flexing, grasping until her short nails bit into her palm. "I hate her, Orren. Can't you get rid of her?"

"Not without a good reason."

"Is *because I hate her* not a good enough reason?"

Orren sat back down, folding his hands on the desk. "Not for Mr. Parker, no." He picked up a pen, passing it back and forth between his hands before setting it back down on the desk. "What happened?"

"She stole that client right out from under me."

"That's not the first time that's happened, why do you seem so much angrier now?"

"It's the way she talks," Max said, leaning against the desk. "Like she's better than everyone else."

"You won't have to deal with her forever."

"No, because I'm going to get fired halfway through the season when I don't get enough clients, because she keeps stealing them all!"

"You know this mountain better than anyone. Better than me, even, and we both know I've been here far longer than I should have." Orren smoothed a paper on his desk, clearing his throat quietly. "Use your knowledge to your advantage. If she talks a better game, then you need to up your own."

"Please, Orren, don't talk to me in platitudes." Max groaned, burying her head in her hands. "What am I going to do?"

"You're going to figure it out. But for now, I need you to leave, because someone just pulled up outside, and we'd better check them into the hotel, rather than scare them away."

"Fine."

"Don't do anything rash, Max." He raised an eyebrow at her. "Don't think that I don't remember the antics you've gotten into over the years."

"Every bit of it was justified."

"I'm not so sure Mr. Parker would agree, when it comes time to make staffing decisions."

Max rolled her eyes. "Really, Orren? You're going to play that card?"

"Whatever keeps you out of trouble. We all know it's your middle name."

"I don't *have* a middle name, so the joke is on you."

"Don't forget the decorating deadline, I don't want to have to explain why it's not done." He sat up straight in his chair, tugging at the dark red fleece he was wearing, emblazoned with the Crimson Oak logo. "Don't set anything on fire."

"Oh, I won't set anything on fire," Max said, heading for the door.

"I don't like how you said that."

"Bye, Orren."

Chapter 4

Sloane trudged back to her cabin from the slopes, her skis tucked under an arm. Amber Pennington might claim to have skied since childhood, but you wouldn't know it by looking at her form. Not just sloppy, but dangerous, and she'd had to intervene at least three times that day.

She ached with the fatigue of a long, harried day, of the constant smile and ever-present social norms that had to be adhered to, alongside a sea of backhanded remarks about nationals disguised as compliments, and the exhaustion dragged at her, even as she crested the final hill to her assigned cabin.

Her stomach clenched as she approached, the slice of yellowed light broaching the wilderness through the open door. It was ajar, and she was alone. Sloane fumbled in her pack for bear spray, pulling it free. She held it out in front of herself as she approached the door. "Hello?" she called into the cabin.

Expecting to find disarray and chaos, overturned bags and drawers that had been rifled though, Sloane was surprised to find the cabin empty and untouched. Shivering in the evening draft, she checked the bathroom, under the bed, and in the closet before she kicked the door closed and locked it, still shaken. She couldn't have left the door standing open when she left that morning, could she?

Closing herself in the bathroom, she stripped, letting steam from the shower graze against the old tiles, sun bleached and dated. She washed, scrubbing the day from her scalp, scraping it from her skin with soap. She braced against the wall, and water almost too hot to stand cascaded over her, and it was almost like drowning just enough to remember to catch her breath. Sloane pressed her palms flat against the tile, tilting her head until; her forehead met porcelain. "Today sucked, but tomorrow will be better," she said aloud.

"Today sucked, but tomorrow will be better." She repeated it twice more as she turned off the water and reached for a towel, finding none. Sloane growled into the empty space, casting a glance around the room. It wasn't in the laundry pile, nor was it hanging up. She harrumphed quietly, shivering as she climbed out of the shower and opened the bathroom door, letting all of the steam dissipate.

Opening the linen closet, she scowled. No towels there, either. What the hell kind of place was Crimson Oak, anyway? Grumbling audibly now, she grabbed the undershirt she'd just stripped off, using it to wick away the droplets of water beading across her skin. It was soaked in a matter of seconds, and she wrung it out over the bathroom sink, along with her hair, dripping ever more frigid moisture into the gently scratched porcelain. The room was freezing, having let all the heat out through the open door, and she shivered violently, rushing to scrape water from her body.

Sloane dug through her bag, willing a towel to appear. Of course, none did, because she'd assumed that any halfway decent lodge would at least have *towels* for their instructors, but apparently not. She pulled out a dry shirt, using that to squeeze her hair out. Rushing to get dressed, she pulled on fresh pajamas, savoring the relative warmth of them, even though it dissipated all too quickly. She hung the drenched clothes up over the shower rail, and they dripped down into the bathtub with quiet, irritatingly rhythmic droplets. She closed the bathroom door to muffle the sound, already too much after what had been a harrowing day.

With a heavy and resigned sigh, she pulled her hair dryer from her bag, plugging it in behind the nightstand and sitting down on top of the comforter.

Moisture immediately wicked up through the blankets and soaked into her pajamas. Sloane leaped up off the bed with an abrupt, swallowed screech, tearing back the comforter to find every towel in her room soaked and left on the bed to seep into the mattress, cold and unwelcoming. She hissed out an angry sigh, glaring at the darkened patches of wet on the sheets.

There were no spare sheets in the closet, not that it would matter. The mattress was soaked through and had the weather been any colder, would have been half-frozen. As it was, she couldn't sleep in it.

What kind of immature, irresponsible little bridge troll would do something like that? An unsupervised child, maybe, running rampant across the lodge. If she'd left her door open, it could have been anyone, any passer-by who wanted to cause some mischief. Stripping down again, she flung her sodden pajamas over the shower rail as well, pulling fresh clothes from her bag.

Sloane slammed the door behind her, angrily marching back to reception and throwing open the door. "Mr. Ralt," she said, surprised at the empty room. "Mr. Ralt?" She peered behind the desk, finding no one. The door to the back room was locked, but through the tiny window she could see that it was empty, too. What kind of lodge left reception unstaffed? She growled under her breath, louder this time, yanking open a closet door, willing there to be spare linens. There wasn't. The closet was filled with file boxes and stationery, and nothing more. A leaf of letterhead floated gently to the floor, emblazoned with the Crimson Oak logo, and she scowled at it before crumpling it up and throwing it back into the closet.

Stalking across the lodge's grounds, she tentatively reached for the door-knob of the laundry room. It was locked. Of course it was locked. She was only supposed to have access some of the time, and late evening wasn't it. Tension settled menacingly between her shoulder blades, and she closed her eyes, willing it to dissipate, but it didn't. It stayed, coiled, rusted, and barbed.

The kitchen was open, but they all stared at her like she was a wild animal that had accidentally found its way inside.

"Uh, hi," Sloane said, tugging at the zipper of her parka, her hair still dripping over her shoulder. "The laundry area was locked, and I was wondering if any of you have keys."

"Who are you?" a woman asked, a hand on her hip, resting against her apron. She was shorter than Sloane and slight, her clothes almost too big for her, and the hairnet sagged against her collar, containing a mess of dark curls.

"Sloane Hearst. I'm the ski instructor."

"We don't have keys here. We're only contractors, and they don't trust us with the keys."

"Who would have keys, then? I have kind of an emergency."

The woman turned back to the counter, skinning potatoes effortlessly, shooting the peels perfectly into the waiting bag. "Orren Ralt would have keys."

"I already tried reception, he's not there."

"Then I can't help you." She looked over her shoulder at Sloane. "And you don't look like you're bleeding, so I'm guessing that *emergency* is a bit of an overstatement."

Sloane sighed heavily, her hand still on the door knob. "Someone got into my cabin and soaked my mattress. They used all the towels in there, and I didn't realize until I was getting out of the shower."

"As much as I wish I could sympathize, the rest of us contractors don't even get on-site accommodations." She frowned, dropping another potato into a pot of water. "Not anymore, anyway. Not since Mr. Parker realized he could make us drive up from town every day."

"Oh." It was all Sloane could think of to say, as she hovered in the doorway.

"Besides, I'm sure you're smart enough to figure this out, but here in the kitchen, we don't have spare linens. I imagine if we did, they'd all start to smell of onions."

"No, I know that, I was just hoping for keys, but you don't have those, so I'll just..." Sloane trailed off. "I'll just go, then."

"It's a good lesson to keep your door locked."

"Obviously."

The woman skinned another potato in record time before turning back to Sloane. "It was probably some kid. These rich—well, certain people come up here and think the lodge is free babysitting. They let their kids run wild, and they get into mischief. You should just be glad that they didn't go through your things." She raised an eyebrow. "They didn't go through your things, right?"

"No, not as far as I can tell."

"Count yourself lucky, then. One year an instructor had his boxers, all of them, strung up the flagpole for everyone to see. He left the next day."

Sloane straightened. "I'm not leaving."

"It doesn't matter one way or the other to me, sweetheart." It may have been a term of endearment, but there was a sharp edge to it that made Sloane uneasy. The woman waved her hand in the air, paring knife grasped between her fingers. "Like I said, there's not much we can do in here that will fix your problems."

"Yeah. Thanks anyway." Sloane pulled the kitchen door shut, standing in the shallow snow, shivering. It wasn't how she'd wanted to start her time at Crimson Oak, especially not that close to the full moon, with the frustration settling into her muscles like hives of wasps, poised for attack. It itched in her bones, and she knew she wasn't far from losing her composure if she wasn't careful.

Hearsts always stayed composed. They were Bears with a long-standing family name, Bears who were leaders for others like them, high achievers despite their curse. Well, if a curse was even what it was. Sloane had never minded it. There was something freeing about running wild through the forest once a month, in a way that the slopes never were. On skis, she had to be measured, controlled, with perfect form and total concentration. In the woods, she was free for one blissful moment.

She went back to reception, still finding it empty. Drumming her fingers against the desk, she had to wonder if Mr. Ralt was in the main hall, on the other side of the lodge. She left, trudging across wet snow, bone-tired and ready to sleep in the ski-tow if it just meant she would be allowed to rest.

The main lodge was impressive at least, with a classic log facade, two stories tall, an edifice that had probably been astounding in its prime. At the moment, it needed some attention, with paint beginning to chip on a few of the shutters, and the steps discolored from probably years of mud. Sloane stepped over the threshold into the main hall, breathing in the warm scent of cinnamon as she took in the grand staircase, somewhat less grand when it was buried beneath dozens of creased boxes.

"Mr. Ralt?" she asked after clearing her throat.

He turned, holding an artificial pine bough in his hand. "Ah, Ms. Hearst.

What can I do for you?"

"I was hoping you had the keys to the laundry. Someone—"

"I'm sorry, Ms. Hearst, maybe I wasn't clear enough about the laundry situation?" He tutted quietly, but with a smile. "Tonight the cleaning staff has access, to wash linens for new arrivals tomorrow that we have booked in."

"I do understand that, it's just that someone broke into my cabin and soaked my mattress through using the towels in there." She gestured at her hair, still dripping. "I didn't realize until I got out of the shower."

"Broke in?" he asked, glancing towards the staff door behind the staircase. "Was the lock compromised?"

"No, I must have left the door open. It was foolish of me, I know, some kid probably got up to mischief. Still, it would be nice if I at least had clean linens to sleep on the floor until the mattress dries out."

He gave her a strange look, opening his mouth to speak, and then swallowing back the words. "I see." With a heavy sigh, he put the decorations down, dusting off his hands. "Unfortunately, I don't have any more spare linens tonight. Maybe in the morning I can get some from the night cleaning crew, but as of right now, I have nothing to offer you."

"I understand."

"I'd recommend keeping your door locked from now on, Ms. Hearst."

Sloane suppressed a groan. "Yes, that much is clear, Mr. Ralt. I am not accustomed to this kind of behavior at a lodge, and it caught me unaware."

"I find it hard to believe that—children—do not get up to no good at other lodges. Children are children, no matter where they are."

"Other lodges tend to have childcare available."

"Be that as it may, Crimson Oak does not offer that service. However, I will feed this back to Mr. Parker, although I do not anticipate it will do much good, where that is concerned."

Max came through the staff door, arms piled high with boxes marked XMAS in red marker. "I found some more lights, Orren, but they're tangled as hell." She caught Sloane's glance and smirked. "Ah, Sloane. Maybe you can help out for once, if you're not too busy stealing clients."

"Unfortunately, I'm busy trying to track down some spare linens. I don't suppose you have any?"

"Fresh out."

"Of course."

Mr. Ralt cleared his throat, taking one of the boxes from Max. "All of us here have a deadline to decorate the main hall here before Mr. Parker shows up with the investors. The festive season is the bread and butter for Crimson Oak, so we need to show it looking its best." He frowned at the tangled ball of lights that he'd just pulled from the box. "We're all expected to help out, so I hope I can count on you to do your part. I understand you were with a client—student—all day, so tonight may not be the best time for you, especially in light of your bed situation."

"You want me to decorate." Sloane phrased it as a statement, not a question. She was a ski instructor, not an interior designer, and this job placement was growing worse and worse by the moment. "I wouldn't even know where to begin."

Max tossed a bundle of garland at her, launching it across the room with far more force than was necessary. "I'm sure you'll figure it out, princess."

Mr. Ralt shot her a look. "Max—"

"If you tell me what needs to be done, I will do it," Sloane interrupted. "I am nothing if not a team player."

"Yeah, so much of a team player that you swanned on in and stole a client out from under me."

"Trust me, I was doing you a favor." The garland was itchy and coarse in her hands, and she frowned at it with disdain. "Amber Pennington is a challenge, if nothing else."

Max scoffed noisily, sucking her teeth. "That should have been my discovery to make. If you try that again, I can guarantee that this isn't going to end well for you."

"Oh yeah? Is that a threat?"

Mr. Ralt cleared his throat. "Ladies—"

"Don't *ladies* me, Orren," Max spat. "She knows what she did."

"I was trying to provide a service to a client," Sloane said evenly. "This lodge is struggling, if you hadn't noticed, and she was already bent out of shape because you were late."

"I wasn't late, I didn't even know she was out there!"

"Regardless, the last thing this place needs is for her to go back to wherever she calls home, spouting off about how terrible this place is. This is the midwest, if you hadn't noticed, and Bear Mountain is hardly a tourist destination like places out west are."

Max rolled her eyes, balancing the remaining boxes on her hip. "It's a fine destination, if you know what you want."

"Most people *don't* know what they want."

"This place was doing just fine without you, Ms. Hearst, and we'll do just fine after you're long gone, flown back to whatever swamp you call home."

Sloane pinned the garland over the door, shoving the tacks in until the base dented the drywall. "You seem to be under the impression that I will be easy to scare off. You are incorrect." She turned, raising an eyebrow at Max in challenge. "I am made of sterner stuff than that." Pushing her wet hair over her shoulder, she marched past Max, taking another box from her. "I'll take this for later."

"Fine." Max's eyes flashed with something almost like recognition, but she blinked, and it was gone. "Suit yourself."

Chapter 5

Orren stood in the doorway of reception, hands on his hips in the mid-morning sun. "I know it was you, Max."

"What was me?" Max asked innocently, propping her board up against the outside of the building. It was another day of slushy snow and slow speeds down the mountain, another day of hustling for clients that weren't there, and it was barely eleven, and she was tired.

"You soaked her mattress."

"I did nothing of the sort. It's not my fault if she leaves her door standing open, inviting all kinds of mischief."

"We had no children on site yesterday," Orren said, looking down at his clipboard. "And given your predisposition to finding trouble wherever you go, it doesn't take a detective to add it all up."

"She deserved it."

"You can't keep doing this, Max."

Max snorted. "You act like I do this every other week. The last time was four years ago, and he was a jerk, and he deserved it, too."

"You're not the arbiter of right and wrong at Crimson Oak," Orren chided. "It's unprofessional."

"And stealing clients out from under me is professional?"

"Having met Ms. Pennington, I think it's safe to say that Sloane wasn't lying when she said she'd done you a favor."

"Yeah," Max said, rolling her eyes dramatically, "doing me so many favors that I'm the one who gets turfed out midway through the season."

"Be better, Max."

"Relax, Orren, I won't continue to antagonize her. It's not like she can handle much more of it without jumping off the deep end. Rich people like her can never handle a little light pranking."

He stepped aside, allowing her entry. "See that it's the case that you stop," he said. "We have enough problems here, especially this season, without you causing more of them."

"She started it."

"Max—"

"Alright, alright," she relented, heading for the coffee pot. "You've made your point. Can we please move on?"

"There's a small group coming in after lunch today, a group of college students it looks like. Two have requested snowboarding, and two requested skiing."

"At the same time?"

He nodded. "Yes, at the same time."

"She's going to be in my way."

"Then pick a different slope."

Max gritted her teeth as she poured the coffee. "That one is the best for beginners and you know it. If I forfeit the good one, she's going to run roughshod over me all season."

"This isn't a war, Max."

"Isn't it?"

"No, it's a winter sports lodge, and we're all here just trying to do our best."

The door jingled, and Sloane entered, looking annoyingly refreshed despite the prank. "Good morning, Mr. Ralt," she said, flipping her silky brunette hair over her shoulder. "Are we still booked in with that group this afternoon?"

Orren nodded. "We are. Simultaneous, half you, and half with Max."

"Did you sleep well?" Max asked with a nonchalant tone.

"Like a baby, once I dried out my mattress with my blow drier. Toasty and warm, perfection, if you ask me." Sloane shot her an empty, winning smile, the kind that was always visible on the covers of magazines. "I trust you will refrain from destroying the piste today, Max?"

"That depends on how terrible your baby skiers are."

"I'm sure they will be doing just fine in no time at all. My students tend to pick things up rather quickly. I imagine they will be on the intermediate slope by tomorrow morning."

Max laughed. "Sure thing, Hearst. We'll see about that."

"Good, I think we will see about that, actually. Maybe you can take notes on how a real instructor behaves."

"A real instructor? I've been teaching here for almost twelve years."

"And yet you still can't manage to be on time, can you? You left poor Ms. Pennington waiting for over twenty minutes. That's hardly what I would call professionalism."

Max glanced at Orren, willing him to react, but he didn't. Coward. "You can have Ms. Pennington for all I care. She only chose you because she wants to pry about how your career went so far off the rails. That's how you people behave."

"You people?"

"Yeah. *You people.* Rich people, with nothing better to do than meddle in each other's lives and gossip behind each other's backs, all the while pretending to be best friends in front of the cameras."

"You're making an awful lot of assumptions about me."

Max shrugged. "Prove me wrong, then."

"Oh, I plan to. In fact, proving you wrong is going to be my top priority, right after proving that skiing is the superior winter sport."

"The only people who think that, are people who've never been on a board in their lives." Max smirked, folding her arms over her chest. "Give it time, I'm sure you'll see the light."

"Mr. Ralt, is there anything else I need to be aware of today? Other clients, groups maybe?"

Orren shook his head. "No, Ms. Hearst. Although, if you get a chance, the deadline for decorations is tomorrow afternoon."

Sloane nodded. "I've already gotten a head start in the main hall, don't you worry about that." She grinned, and it was threatening in the way that mean girls in the halls of every high school were threatening. Saccharine, laced with rot and thorns. "I will be finishing up later, before dinner."

"No plans tonight?" Max asked. "No desire to go roaming around the old trails?"

"In the dark? No." Sloane shifted the skis under her arms. "Much as you may be desperate to get rid of me, Carter, I'm not so foolish as to willingly throw myself off the side of the mountain."

"Full moon tonight. Might be nice and bright, if the clouds don't settle in." Max tilted her chin, watching for a reaction. There was something off about Sloane Hearst, but she couldn't quite figure it out. "No moonlit walks for you, then?"

"No."

"It isn't advisable, even without the usual levels of snow," Orren agreed, sitting down in his chair. "You know better than that, Max."

"I know this mountain better than I know my own mother," Max said. A truth, but not a hard one to achieve, considering her family's deeply fractured dynamics. "Better than I know myself, even."

"See you on the slopes," Sloane said, ignoring her. As she went, Max silently cursed herself for watching her go, her curves a frustratingly interesting silhouette against the landscape. Damned skiers.

* * *

Max stripped off her parka, dropping it into a box outside the tow line. It was warm, too warm for nearly December. The slopes were already a mess of slush and sludge, even with the limited guest numbers at the lodge. If things didn't cool off soon, they were in for a lean winter, and one where Mr. Parker would win, and they'd all lose.

"Welcome to Crimson Oak," she said, holding her hand out to the group. They all shook it, in turn. "I'm Max, I'll be the snowboard instructor today. Who am I taking on?"

Two raised their hands, a boy and a girl, probably nineteen years old. They were holding hands, and it would have been cute if Max hadn't spent the past four years being reticently single. She forced a smile at them and held her arms out with enthusiasm. "Great!"

33

"What about us?" the other two asked, a similar age, but already looking bored.

"I'm not sure where your instructor is, she's usually so punctual." Smugness seethed in her, and she let it. "Let me see if I can find her. Are you two okay for a moment if I do that?"

The couple nodded, too enamored with each other to even notice.

Max set off towards the staff cabins, ready to rip into Sloane when she found her. So much for her big, irritating speech about providing a service, or whatever it was that she'd said. "Hey!" she called, approaching Sloane's cabin. It was no wonder they'd given her the nicer cabin, with the bigger bed, and the brighter windows. "You're late, Ms. Hearst, your clients are waiting for you."

Sloane skidded through the door, slamming it behind her and locking it. "I'm aware, thank you."

"What's the matter, you take a nap or something? Slept through your alarm?"

"I wasn't taking a nap, I was working up at the main hall, and then I realized I'd forgotten something in my cabin. I'm only three minutes late."

"Three minutes can feel like an eternity to a client, wouldn't you agree?"

"Do you ever let up?" Sloane asked, pulling her hair back into a messy ponytail. It was a far cry from the sleek braid she'd had the day before. "I mean, really, do you ever give it a rest? Or are you like this twenty-four seven?"

"I'm always like this." Max turned, heading back towards the tow line. "Especially when provoked."

"I didn't provoke you."

"Sure thing, princess."

Sloane's footsteps behind were uneven, struggling to catch up. "Stop calling me that."

"I will, when you stop acting like one. How did you get the nicer cabin, anyway? Throw a tantrum, maybe stomp your foot on the ground until Mr. Parker caved?"

"I didn't request any kind of specific accommodation, thank you very much.

I am housed where they decided to put me. I was made aware, however, that you insisted on having your cabin all to yourself."

"You have your own cabin, too," Max shot back. "That's hardly a condemnation."

"My point is, you're the one with the demands, not me."

"I've been here for twelve years, it's literally the least they could do, given the bottom-grade level of pay we get." She glared at Sloane out of the corner of her eye. "At least, I'm assuming we have the same pay structure, although given it's you, princess of the piste, it wouldn't surprised me if they'd offered you double what I make."

"I wasn't offered anything special."

"That you know of, maybe." Max waved at the group, giving them a thumbs-up and gesturing to Sloane. "I found her!" she called across the snow. "She forgot!"

"I didn't forget," Sloane hissed.

"She forgot all about you!"

"Carter, if you don't stop—"

Max grinned, clapping a hand on the boy's shoulder. "Are you ready to learn snowboarding?"

He nodded carefully, but his girlfriend was eagerly bouncing on the balls of her feet already. Max loved an eager learner, and couldn't wait to get them on the slopes. "Okay, today we're going to learn the basics, unless either of you already has some experience?"

They both shook their heads, and Max looked to the other two. "What about you, any skiing experience?"

"I hate skiing," one of the girls said. "I'm only here because they made me. I wanted to go to Cabo San Lucas for winter break, but no, we're here instead."

Max swallowed back a snort. "Alright, well, Sloane, I'll leave these two in your capable hands. Good luck!"

"I hope you can manage to resist the urge to destroy the piste," Sloane shot back. "It makes my job harder when you're busy teaching people how to carve chunks out of it, and it's even worse in this slush."

"You really need to come up with a better line," Max said brightly, aware that the group was still watching them, "or people will start to think you don't even know how to ski in these conditions."

"Of course I—I was almost to nationals!"

"Wait so you're like, famous or something?" one of the skiers asked, pulling out her phone. "Can we get a picture for socials before we start?"

"I'm not—I don't—" Sloane said, backing away. "We should just get going, it's already past the time we should be getting you into some skis."

"I'd have thought you loved the limelight," Max said, leaning against the control shed. "After all, you've been on the cover of Winter Sports Magazine twice now."

"I had to, because of my sponsors," Sloane muttered, turning her back to the camera. "I don't like cameras."

The girl holding the phone made a loud tsk noise and put it back into her pocket. "I knew we should have gone to Cabo. At least there, I'd get a tan. At least there, I could be laying on the beach, not standing on top of a mountain."

"Oh my gosh, Mackenzie, shut up," the other skier said. "You're always so *negative.*"

"I'm not negative, I'm expressing my truth."

Max cleared her throat to hide a laugh and pulled gear from the shed. "Right, boarders, follow me to the bunny slope and we'll get you started, how does that sound?"

The young couple followed her, the girl hustling to keep up with Max's quick pace. "How long have you been snowboarding?"

"Since I was thirteen," Max answered. "What are your names?"

"I'm Alison, this is Jake. I'm so excited to be here, I've always wanted to try this. I just love winter, and I've watched so many videos online, do you know how to do tricks?"

"I do, but I don't know that we'll get there for you today, it would be a lot to cover in one lesson."

"How many lessons would I need?"

"It depends on the person. Some people take to snowboarding quicker than others."

"Jake, do you think we could stay a few extra days? I really want to try at least one jump. It's all I want to do this trip."

"I dunno, Ally, Mackenzie and Nell don't seem that happy to be here."

"Yeah, but we always do what they want to do, it's why we wound up in Vegas on Christmas last year, and that Elvis impersonator kept following us down the strip. Come on, isn't it nicer here? At least there's snow, and the cabins are cute, and—"

Jake sighed, following behind her. "I have to get back to work in a few days."

"One extra day, then."

Max approached the top of the bunny slope, laying the borrowed boards on the ground. "You could always stay yourself, you know. You don't need your friends or your..." she gave Alison a questioning look. "Boyfriend?"

"Yeah."

"You don't need them, if you really wanted to stay."

"Yeah, Ally, you should just stay if you want to." Jake strapped himself to the board, following Max's lead. "If it's important, stay. I'll be waiting for you when you get back." He straightened, wobbling for a moment. "I just can't be around Mackenzie more than a few days."

Alison laughed, already standing upright, strapped in. "Oh, she's just a brat. I still love her, she comes in clutch, you know? Like that time my car broke down in the middle of the night on that creepy highway, she got out of bed and came to save me."

"You could have called me, you know," Jake said, clearly uncomfortable with the board.

Alison laughed, slapping her knee. "You don't even wake up when there's a tornado alarm."

"Alright," Max said, preparing to guide them through some basic movements, "let's get started."

Chapter 6

The moon was oppressively bright, sending a cold glow to cascade down across the mountain, prickling the tips of the pine trees, filtering down into the murky depths of the woods. It was cold, though not as cold as it should have been that time of year, so Sloane waited in a small clearing, hanging jeans, an undershirt, and a padded vest from a low-hanging branch.

She left her boots until the last, hating the way it felt to stand on half-frozen, muddy ground. Despite being what she was, feeling cold earth squish up through her toes was possibly the worst feeling she could imagine, and it made her want to climb up into the limbs, knowing they'd snap as soon as she turned. Most trees couldn't handle the weight of an eight foot Bear, and the ones that could, rarely had branches low enough. Besides, climbing down after she turned was almost impossible, and she knew this, because she'd tried it at least half a dozen times.

It dragged at her skin, a pull that was inescapable but freeing. As a Bear, the day to day worries that plagued her, the effort of maintaining an appropriate public face, was mitigated. She wished the full moon lasted longer than one or two nights; she'd spend her entire life as a bear if she could, solitary and calm. No one to impress, no coaches pushing her past her limits, no family gatherings where they'd all look at her with expressions of pity for falling short of what she'd been meant to be.

Shifting was a delicate freedom, and one that Sloane had cherished ever since the first time, when she was twelve. She'd known it was coming, both her parents were Bears, and all four of her grandparents, and when it had finally happened, it filled her with such a sense of release that she vowed then and there to spend all her time in the woods, on mountains, bathing in snow and pine needles and the blue light of the moon at its peak.

Feeling the shift begin as the moon approached its peak, she kicked off her boots, flinging them over the branch to hang by the double-knotted laces. She grimaced at the feel of the snow against the soles of her feet, but as bone and sinew elongated, manipulated themselves beneath her skin, she allowed the Bear to wash over her like a cleansing rain after a drought, or a hot shower after a hard run.

Her skin burned as fur sprouted from every follicle, until the Sloane the rest of the world knew was barely visible at all. She was hidden, in a sense, despite her eight foot frame and the fact that polar bears were certainly not native to Michigan's upper peninsula. She was off the trails, buried deep in the woods where no one would find her, and for the first time since she'd arrived at Crimson Oak, she breathed deep, inhaling and exhaling, intentional and necessary.

Somewhere, a wolf howled at the moon, and it tingled along her spine, as though she was pulled to it. She'd known there would probably be a few on the mountain, they weren't unheard of in the area, but while she'd always gone out of her way to avoid contact with any other animals, be they Weres or not, she found herself padding through the woods, heading for the sound.

Another howl and a part of her wished she could howl, too. It had been so long since she'd had a shift so freeing. The last one had been spent sedated in a hotel room, hiding from the press who all wanted to know why the up-and-coming Sloane Hearst had pulled out of qualifiers. There weren't many places to run that close to a city, not given her size and the amount of photographers running around. Someone finding a polar bear in Colorado would make the news, and she'd wind up in the basement of some government laboratory.

Bears were everywhere, but they had to be careful. Most people would go out of their way to kill a Bear, thinking it was a normal bear, and then the cover-up was always a nightmare, with her family, or a few others, being the ones who footed the bill for it, to keep them all safe, to keep all their secrets.

The pine needles glistened in the moonlight, the damp of the melting snow both ominous and beautiful, like so many things in life. A threat, but attractive. Like Max. She shook her head, irritated that her mind was so full with problems from her human life. Usually, a shift dampened all of that, letting her wander, suppressing the intrusive thoughts that never seemed to leave her alone for very long. The forest was the only place she could escape it.

The moon climbed higher in the star-pricked sky, a deep, silken blue that was almost black. This far from the city, the constellations were allowed to shine bright, flickering through years of time and space. The starry glimmers had left their source years before, when she was younger, more innocent. It was always strange, looking up at light that had been created before she'd been born.

Sloane stopped, sitting back on her haunches as she bathed in the glow of it. She was warm, and longed for a slab of ice, but settled for the dribbles of melting icicles that adorned the branches above her head. The wolf howled again, and once more she felt pulled towards the sound. It was strange that she had no other sense of it, no scent. Under normal conditions, she'd smell a wolf miles off, but this one must be much closer than that. Maybe she was getting sick, maybe congestion in her sinuses was dampening her ability to track.

The mountain's slope was more jagged, more abrupt as she approached the sound, and nearly stumbled twice as she climbed. Polar Bears weren't meant for climbing, not with their enormous size. Part of her longed for the ocean, but those were growing ever more dangerous with every passing year. Overfishing was only one of the myriad of problems they were facing, and the Bears of the north had begun to scatter across the continents, looking for better places, colder, more remote, more freedom, more solitude.

A wolf stood at the peak's crest, snout poised up at the sky. It howled once more, the eerie sound echoing across the valley like a warning. Sloane stayed where she was, watching from beneath the relative safety of an overhead tree. It was like no wolf she'd ever seen, beautifully colored with silver and grey, and it was enormous. Not as large as she was herself, but for a wolf, the size was almost intimidating.

Sloane snuffled quietly, pawing through the slush. There were no tracks to hunt, but she'd left herself a pile of salmon, twelve full-sized fish she'd bought the day before at the town twenty miles away. It was not where she'd left it. The stash was gone, the only proof she had left any there in the first place being couple of discarded fish tails.

She batted at the remaining snow angrily, willing the rest to present themselves, despite knowing that whatever had found her little cache had eaten well, and eaten all of it. With nothing else on the mountain to eat, or at least, nothing she wanted to consider eating, her stomach growled angrily, and she laid down on the ground, defeated.

The wolf padded down from the peak, still unaware of her presence. In its mouth was a fat, pink salmon, a prize it had won from the earth, not questioning what a pile of fish was doing so far from the sea. Sloane stood again, so abruptly that it alerted the wolf to her presence under the canopy of pine.

It jerked in surprise, clamping down on the fish. Sloane roared, and it was instinct, impulse, a dangerous one if someone decided to investigate. The wolf backed up, stumbling on its huge paws, still holding the fish in its mouth. Sloane opened her mouth to roar again, but the wolf took off running through the trees, so graceful that it hardly left tracks behind itself.

She'd never catch it, not with her size, and the difficult terrain, and the fact that despite how much she desperately craved the taste of fish, she didn't relish the idea of a fight with a wolf. Where there was one, there were probably others, and that was a scuffle she didn't want to experience, even if she won. It wasn't worth one fish. One measly salmon was hardly going to put a dent in her hunger.

Sloane laid down on the cold ground yet, cold but not frozen, and thus too warm for her layers of fat and fur that pushed into the mud, leaving an impression in the earth that would likely confuse passers-by, if they were foolish enough to wander off the trails. It wouldn't be the first time someone blamed a strange Were sighting on a cryptid, nor would it be the last.

Blame it on Bigfoot, and no one would really even care what it had been in the first place. Hell, there was a whole den of Polar Bears up in Canada who regularly baited the townspeople into yeti sightings. It was a whole tourist charade that no one took seriously, and they hid in plain sight. A good plan, if you had enough space to roam.

Her stomach rumbled again, and she groaned, which had a strangely familiar sound through her Bear's throat. It was going to be a long damned night without food, with nothing to hunt up this way, not even a herd of deer, and she'd have a hard time getting extra rations from the kitchen in the morning to make up for it.

* * *

Sloane yawned for the sixth time in five minutes, leaning against the kitchen door. She was so greedily hungry that in the moments before the cook arrived, she was considering ripping off a chunk of tree bark to chew on. At least the unpleasant earthiness would be a distraction from the pinched pangs in her gut.

"Morning," the cook said, approaching the door. "You're early."

"I have some clients first thing," Sloane lied. "Just trying to get a jump on the day, you know how it is."

"Nothing is ready as of yet."

"I know, if I could get fruit or something, even that would be a huge help."

"I've only got canned, we haven't gotten the new delivery yet. Will be a few hours, yet."

Sloane swallowed hard, dreading the metallic taste even before it was in her mouth. She offered what she hoped was a smile. "Sure, that would be great."

"What's with your face?"

"Oh, nothing, just tired."

The woman's brow furrowed before she turned, unlocking the door. "You're Sloane Hearst, right?"

"I am."

"I doubt you'll have heard of me, unless there are magazines highlighting catering contractors."

"Maybe there should be. This place wouldn't run without you."

"I'm Bev Jones." She held out a hand, shaking Sloane's. "Your type doesn't usually want to associate with us here in the kitchen."

"I'm not silly enough to piss off where my food comes from."

"Coffee?"

Sloane nodded. "Please."

"Make it then. Grounds are in the top cabinet, there." Bev gave a vague gesture to the corner of the kitchen, tying an apron around her waist. "Better make enough for everyone, so do a full pot."

Sloane nodded, closing the door behind her. She measured the grounds into a filter, counting each one as she dumped it in. The rich aroma twinged her stomach, and bile burned in her throat from the emptiness. She swallowed back a retch, covering her mouth with the back of her hand.

"You alright?" Bev asked, hand poised over a bowl with an egg in her hand, ready to crack.

"I'm fine."

"You're not pregnant, are you?" Bev set the egg down, her eyes wide. "Oh, honey. You must be pregnant. That would explain you pulling out of qualifiers."

Sloane tried to laugh, but it came out strangled and strange. "No, definitely not pregnant. Just a... rough night."

Bev raised an eyebrow. "If you say so."

"I find it hard to sleep in new places."

"I imagine that's magnified by someone breaking into your cabin, no?"

"It hasn't helped," Sloane answered. "Lesson learned, I guess."

"Have you met Mr. Parker yet?"

"No. Should I have?"

"I suppose that depends on your perspective." Bev cracked three more eggs in quick succession, dumping them into the bowl and setting the empty shells aside. "This place has been going downhill for years. I think he just wants to be rid of it now."

"Why? It has so much potential."

"Effort, for one thing. Interested investors, for another. Easier to sell it and wash his hands of the whole thing than to invest in a reinvention. Rumor has it some scout from Syndicorp is here to scope the place out."

Sloane kept her eyes fixed on the coffee as it dripped into the pot. "That's a shame. Those corporate lodges have no soul."

"I thought your type liked that kind of thing."

"I don't know, I guess it depends. My parents like it, sure. White and grey and mid-century modern, everything branded to death." Sloane sighed, pressing her palms flat against the counter. "It's not for me. I'd rather live in a cabin in the forest, given the opportunity."

"Turkey bacon?" Bev asked absent-mindedly, whisking the eggs.

"If you're offering." Sloane's stomach growled again, and she wasn't quite sure she'd make it the twenty minutes it would take for food to be ready.

"I heard that." Bev laughed, tossing a tin of peaches at her. "Here, satiate yourself for the moment. I know a hangover when I see one."

"Something like that." Sloane tore at the ring pull, diving into the juice with her bare hands. Bev wasn't wrong, the morning after a hard shift was a little like a hangover. Everything was foggy, and the day would pass slowly until it was time to try again. "Do you know if anyone is heading into town today? I wanted to ask if they could pick something up at the shop for me."

"I'm going later, if you're not busy. What is it you need?"

"Oh just..." Sloane trailed off, trying not to think about the metallic taste in her mouth. "Just some personal things." The peaches slid down her throat into her stomach, and for a moment she wasn't sure if it was making her feel better or worse. "Nothing serious."

"I'll head off around two, then, if you want to go. But I'm not waiting around forever, I have work that needs doing."

"I'll be there."

Bev turned up the flame under the bacon, and it began to sizzle and pop. The smell was making Sloane feral, like she was about to jump over the counter and devour the rest of it raw. She swallowed hard, reminding herself that her human constitution couldn't handle raw meat, no matter how hungry she'd been as a Bear. Bev nodded towards the walk-in refrigerator. "Make yourself useful, grab the juice and start filling carafes."

"How many guests are on site?"

"Enough."

"Is it slow, would you say? I have no benchmark, I've never been here before."

"Oh, you know." Bev poured buttermilk into a bowl, mixing it into a floury mixture. "Every place like this has its ups and downs. There's no accounting for this weather, though. That's certainly not helping things."

"How long have you been here?"

"What is this, the inquisition?"

Sloane swallowed the final peach, turning to rinse out the can and place it into the recycling. "It just seems like a nice place to stay. The mountain is pretty, and the sky out this far is pretty astounding."

"Three, maybe four years now, it's hard to keep track. Not as long as Max."

Sloane didn't say anything. She turned her focus to the refrigerator, pulling oversized cartons from the shelves. "It's strange that it's been so warm."

Bev laughed. "Wow, you really don't like her, do you?"

"She doesn't make it easy."

"Does anyone?"

"Hmm." Sloane began filling the carafes, focusing on keeping her grip steady so she didn't spill any.

"There's always a little bit of rivalry between instructors here. When I first started here, there were teams, three instructors a side. Max always did her damndest to make sure the ones with attitude problems sent themselves packing."

"She can try whatever she likes, I don't give up that easily."

"Maybe this is the year she finally meets her match." Bev turned the kneaded dough out onto a floured surface, pressing it into a wide rectangle. "So, Sloane Hearst, sweetheart of Winter Sports Magazine, what's your story, anyway? Why the hell are you all the way out here at Crimson Oak?"

Sloane grimaced, setting aside the now empty carton, the juice decanted into the sparkling clean glass carafes. "It's a long story."

"We've got time."

"I don't really want to talk about it."

"Okay." Bev shrugged, cutting discs out of the dough and brushing them with butter. "I get it. But listen, one path isn't the end all, be all, you know what I mean?"

"No, I don't think I do."

"You've been doing this your whole life, right?"

"Pretty much."

"Did you ever consider doing anything else?"

"Oh." Sloane cracked the seal on a new carton. Her jaw was set firm, and she frowned at the droplet of orange that was preparing to drip onto the counter. "I've honestly never thought about it very much before."

"Maybe you should."

"It's not that simple, I have... expectations, I guess, and I'm not ready to throw all of that away."

"I'm just saying, sometimes our first run at a life plan doesn't work out. Sometimes the second and third don't, either, but that's okay." Bev arranged the buttered discs in a circular dish before beginning to cut more. "Life is short, but it's all we'll know. Might as well keep trying to get it right. Hell, I went to school for seven years, and right at the end of it, realized it wasn't going to be for me."

She gestured with a floured hand, waving through the air with a fine dust trailing after her. "I struggled along for a good while, trying to make it work. In the end, I almost lost everything before I would give it up. My family, my husband, my friends, they were all so tired of my shit."

Sloane laughed, covering her mouth with the back of her hand. "Tired of your shit?"

"Oh, I was miserable. Took it out on everyone around me, and for what? For a little more in my bank account? For prestige?" Bev shook her head. "It wasn't worth it. Not for me, anyway." She slid the pan into the oven and bent to wash her hands, scraping off the bits of excess dough. "Maybe it will be the same for you. What do you like doing?"

"I don't know if anyone has ever asked me that before."

"Then you should start asking yourself." Bev dried her hands on her apron, turning back to the pan of bacon to flip each slice with a pair of metal tongs. "If there's one thing I've learned in my five decades on this earth, it's that no one else is going to do the work to unpick all the crap in our brains. It's up to us, unfortunate as that may be."

"It's easier to not deviate."

"Easier maybe, but is it fulfilling? Or are you going to wake up in ten years and wonder what the hell you've been doing this whole time? Asking yourself why you wasted so much time being miserable, when you could have just grabbed life by the guts and chosen something different for yourself."

"Hmm," Sloane mumbled again, and even the thought of it was making panic nestle uncomfortably between her ribs.

Chapter 7

Max stumbled out of bed and into the bathroom, opening one eye to stare blearily at her own reflection. "Ugh," she grunted, pulling two small twigs from her short-cropped hair. She was achy and tired, but it was the kind of gentle exhaustion after a challenging hike, so she stretched her arms over her head and exhaled, savoring the quiet pop of her shoulders.

Tugging on fresh clothes, ones not caked in mud, she ran a brush through her hair to little avail. "Nice, Carter," she mumbled at herself, pulling on a hat. It was one nice thing about winter, not having to worry so much about what her hair looked like.

The door's lock latched with a click behind her, and she trudged across alarmingly green-tinged snow to reception. "Morning, Orren."

"Did you see the forecast?" he asked, a newspaper unfolded in front of his face.

"No signal up here."

"Right, of course." He laid the paper down, his brow furrowed. "They're saying fifty-five, maybe even sixty degrees for the next few days."

"Damn."

"I've already called Mr. Parker and told him we'll have to get the machines fired up at night, but I don't know how much good it will do. The snow will just melt as soon as the sun hits it."

"What a start to December," Max said, collapsing into the chair across from him. "I guess I can't expect any clients for the rest of the week, then."

"Probably not." He eyed her with suspicion. "Rough night?"

"Someone's baiting up near the peak again."

"What?"

Max sighed. "I went for a hike last night, you know, to clear my head, and there was a huge bucket of salmon up there."

"Who even has access all the way up here?"

"I don't know, last time this happened, it was locals from down the mountain a ways. They get up here at night, park at the bottom of the hill, and bait the woods. Damned fools think bagging a predator will make them more manly."

"Are you sure?"

"Who else is leaving buckets of salmon that far off the trails, Orren?"

He folded the paper closed, leaning against the desk. "I didn't think there were many wolves left up this way."

"There aren't. Only a few. When I first came here you'd hear at least six all howling now and then, but now it's only one, maybe two. It's hard to know unless you see them."

"If there are people trying to bait and hunt wolves, we'd better tell the sheriff."

Max snorted. "Please, as if that old bag of bones is going to do anything. Hell, he'd probably join them, given half the chance."

"What, then? Are you going to patrol the woods every night, and wander in here every morning looking like something chewed you up and spat you out?"

"Wonderful." Max rolled her eyes, pouring herself a cup of coffee. "You're out of sugar."

"You want sugar, you can go to the kitchen. That's where you're supposed to be getting it."

"But then I'd miss your irresistible witty banter, and I'd never forgive myself for it."

Orren took the coffee pot from her, topping up his own. "Did you get the main hall finished?"

"No," Max groaned, smacking herself on the forehead. "I forgot."

"Mr. Parker is going to be here this afternoon, you'd better get a move on. We'll have an even harder time convincing him to keep this place open this season with the weather being what it is."

"Alright, fine, I hear you." Max sat back in the chair, cupping her hands around the mug. "I'll go as soon as I finish this."

"You're impossible, Carter."

"Come on, when have I ever let you down before?" She waited for him to respond, arching an eyebrow when he didn't. "That's what I thought."

"You're going to get the both of us fired."

"Fired now or fired at the end of the week, what's the difference?"

"An extra three days of pay is the difference." Orren sighed, closing his eyes against the errant sunbeam escaping the blinds. "Maybe those wolf baiters will be someone else's problem soon."

"Oh, no, I'll keep them as my problem, don't worry."

"You have some kind of weird vendetta against poachers?"

Max shot him a look over the rim of her Crimson Oak branded mug. "After someone nearly got shot five years back? Yes, I'd say I have a vendetta." She sighed heavily. "Those jerks were never caught, either, so for all we know it's the same band of meatheads as before."

"We at least have to tell Mr. Parker. We're duty bound to—"

"Fine, whatever," Max interrupted, waving him away. "It's not like he's going to care anyway."

"No," Orren replied. "Probably not."

"I suppose I can safely assume that I don't have any bookings today?"

"None, I'm afraid.

"Figures." She played with the zip on her parka. "I really thought I'd convinced that one student to stay a few extra days."

"It's a good opportunity to get started on the main hall though, wouldn't you agree? You have all the time in the world to get it done." He checked his watch with a grimace. "Well, all the time in the world looks a little more like four hours, but you get the idea."

"I don't know why we have to put all this crap up anyway. We're just going to take it all down in a month."

"Where's your festive enthusiasm?"

"It died, along with half my paycheck. Cooked to death in these damned late spring temperatures." Max took a sip from her mug, frowning at the bitter liquid. "This actually tastes terrible without sugar. You must be suffering in here, Orren."

"I'm fine with black coffee, thank you."

"Let me go get you sugar from the kitchen, I promise you'll appreciate it."

He smirked at her, rolling his eyes. "You only want me to keep sugar in here for your own specific benefit."

"You can't at least let me pretend it's altruism?"

"Not on your life, Carter."

"A little sugar never killed anyone, you know."

Orren laughed, sipping at his coffee. "I like my coffee how I like my women. Bitter and likely to significantly shorten my lifespan."

"That sounds like a you problem."

"Not a problem for me." He glanced at the clock hanging on the wall, buried beneath a fine coating of dust that gave an irritating sheen in the morning light. "You're going to have problems, though, if you don't get that main hall finished."

"Alright, alright, I hear you, no need to drive it home." Max drained her mug and stood, setting it on the desk. "Why don't you come with me, and you can tell me where stuff needs to go?"

"Just fill in the gaps."

"I am not a decorator, Orren. If you give me vague instructions, I can basically guarantee you aren't going to enjoy the results."

"Garland on the banisters, lights on top. Tree, ornaments. Done."

"Will you just take five minutes, please?" Max pouted. "I hate this decorating stuff, I'm not good at it, and being honest, I don't care about it, either. It's not like we're going to have many guests at the resort to even notice that it's there, not with this weather we're having."

"You never know, it could snow tomorrow for all you know and surprise us all."

"I doubt it."

"It doesn't matter how the decorations get up, Max, just staple them up. You're over thinking this. Mr. Parker just wants to see it done, and given you've waited until moments before the deadline, the time to be picky about it has passed."

"It's not moments before the deadline, you said I had four hours. That means I have three and a half more hours before I have to worry about it."

"Max," he groaned.

"If you come with me, I'll start right away. Come on, Orren, you know me, I hate this stuff. Throw me a bone."

"Fine," he replied, drawing out the syllable. "I really shouldn't be leaving the desk untended, though."

"Oh, because reception is so busy right now?" Max threw an arm out, gesturing wildly at the empty room. "Yeah, I don't know how you'd ever manage to catch up with these record numbers. Hell, we might even have to fire up the no vacancy sign at the base of the mountain at this rate."

"Well, there's no need for that level of sarcasm, is there?"

"I can't help it, it's my default state of being." She waited for him by the door, a hand on the door knob. "Besides, it's part of my charm. Probably the only reason you let me come mooch coffee from you every morning."

He followed her out of reception, turning to lock the door behind them. Orren looked up at the cloudless sky, shading his eyes from the bright sunlight. "I've never seen it like this in December. I remember when the snow would be knee-high before Thanksgiving even hit."

"Those days are long gone, I'm afraid." Max frowned at the rivulets of water running down the sidewalk, the casualty of melting snow. "Who knows if we'll even get them back."

"Maybe they'll turn Crimson Oak into one of those corporate retreats, what do you think?"

"I think that would be a real indictment of where the world is headed, Orren. Who the hell needs another sanitized, bland, rotting carcass of a corporate center? No one needs that, I promise you. Plus, this place is like three hours from the airport. Are they really expecting people to drive in?"

"Maybe they plan to run a shuttle service."

Max sighed, pressing a hand to her forehead. "Probably. Hell, if I get my license upgraded over the summer, maybe I can get a job here ferrying rich assholes to and from the airport. I'm sure that definitely won't make me want to tuck and roll when I'm doing eighty on the highway."

"The speed limit is seventy-five, Carter."

"Yeah but the sooner I got here, the sooner I'd have them off the shuttle. Bus. Van. Whatever."

Orren gave her a concerned look, grasping the tarnished brass of the main hall's handle. "You worry me, Max. Don't be driving like that."

"Only when I'm avoiding awkward conversation. It's why I prefer to drive alone."

"Just because you're a speed demon on the slopes, doesn't mean you should be doing that on the roads."

"It was a joke, Orren."

He pulled the door open and let loose a tiny gasp. "I thought you said you hadn't done anything for the decorations yet."

"I didn't," Max replied, stepping around him to take in the view herself. She sucked in a breath, taking a step back. "Wow."

Intricate paper snowflakes, folded from paper so thin it was almost translucent, sparkled as they hung from the rafters, twisting gently in the undetectable breeze, rotating lazily and showing off the artistry of whoever had made them. The banisters were wound with fresh pine boughs that filled the entire main hall with the heady scent of pine and earth, and twinkling lights were strung across the landing, cascading down over the plush sofas that sat in the main area.

"This is amazing," Orren breathed, turning to examine the tree. The night before, it had been bare, looking lopsided and ready to topple over, but now it was adorned with ornaments of red and gold, just like the Crimson Oak logo, with sprigs of holly tucked neatly between branches, and lit with thousands of tiny lights, delicate on their strands, each of them emitting a warm glow.

"Did Mr. Parker hire a decorator?" Max asked.

"I don't think so, at least, if he did, he didn't tell me about it."

"Maybe he's trying to replace us earlier than we thought."

Orren brushed his fingers against one of the scarlet glass baubles, so gently as to not disturb it. "These have been in storage for years."

"I've not seen the place dressed up like this since I first came here." Max sat in an overstuffed chair, looking up at the lights hanging from the ceiling. "I hope I'm not the one who has to take all this shit down. Is that *real* pine?"

"It makes this place really look like something special, don't you think?"

"Too bad no one is going to see it."

"Not with that attitude, they won't."

Max rolled her eyes. "Does my sarcasm control the weather, now?"

"Look, even the fireplace got the festive treatment." He pointed at the brick against the wall, adorned with holly and lights draped elegantly at the sides. "I wish I could work from here. Or do you think he'd get the decorator to do reception, too?"

"I think you're expecting way too much," Max said with a snort. "I can't even believe we got this much." She leaned back in the chair, bracing her head with her interlaced fingers. "I can't say I'm disappointed that I don't have to do this."

"You're very irritating when you get your way, you know."

"I've been told that before."

"I wonder if they did the gardens, too." Orren headed for the back door, and Max followed, recalcitrant, longing for the soft comfort of the chair.

"Who'd be out in the gardens this time of year? Unseasonably warm weather or no, it's not exactly a paradise." She yawned, and when she opened her eyes to the outside, she stepped back. "Whoa."

"This would have taken hours, how could I not have realized? They must have been here all yesterday, but everything looked normal when I closed up last night." He snorted. "Do you think your poachers might also be the nighttime decorators?"

"I doubt that they'd do any decorating unless it could be done with a rifle, and as far as I'm aware, you can't shoot lights onto the walls." Max leaned against the exterior brick, admiring the newly-trimmed hedges covered in a net of lights that matched those edging the canvas canopies over the tables. "This is a professional job. What the hell is Mr. Parker up to?"

"Same thing he's always up to, I expect, getting a better price for this place before he bows out. A little razzle dazzle can really move the needle if investors are motivated."

"Yeah, I don't know how motivated they'll be when they see the guest numbers and the fact that ninety percent of these rooms are unoccupied."

"Give it time, Max. You're always so impatient."

"I get bored, otherwise." She took a few steps into the garden, walled off on all sides by the tall, thick hedges. "This could almost be used for private parties, if someone wanted. It looks that good."

"Maybe this place does have a future as a corporate retreat lodge."

Max made a retching gesture as she turned back to him. "Don't even say that aloud."

"You can't fight the tide of the inevitable, only ride it."

"That's a little defeatist."

"I'm not a defeatist," Orren said. "I'm a realist. I'd rather work here under the thumb of new corporate overlords than not work here at all."

"I know what you mean." Max sighed, brushing her hair back. "I can't stop thinking about what it might mean for all of us here. I just wish things could go back to the way they were. Skiing, snowboarding, lodge. That's it. No corporate retreats, no damned poachers in the woods, no ski instructors with their heads so far up their—"

"Mr. Ralt!" Sloane said, appearing from behind one of the hedges. She shot a look at Max. "I was going to come grab you from reception when I finished."

Orren stared. "*You* did this?"

"I did. You said the deadline was this afternoon, right? I didn't get that wrong?"

"No, that's right." He raised an appreciative eyebrow. "Ms. Hearst, this place looks astoundingly fantastic. How did you manage to do this all yourself?"

"I didn't sleep much last night."

"Is your mattress still damp?"

Sloane shook her head. "No, just a little keyed up, I think. Tried to make good use of my time."

"I'll say. I can't believe you got all this done so quickly."

"I'm glad you like it. Do you think Mr. Parker will be pleased?"

"I think he will accuse me of going wildly over budget, and then he will be pleased when he learns I did not." Orren ran his hands over a pine bough on the back of a chair. "Did you harvest these from the woods?"

"I didn't cut any down, if that's what you mean. I just collected what was already on the ground. In a forest that dense, it wasn't hard to find plenty that still looked nice."

"It's wonderful."

Max rolled her eyes. "Yeah, yeah, fantastical, now can I go?"

"I'm sorry you didn't get to help," Sloane said sweetly, her tone so saccharine that Max was sure she'd heard everything she'd said since walking into the main hall. Sloane smiled at her as she threaded more lights from one side of the small garden to the other. "Mr. Ralt will just have to tell Mr. Parker that you were sleeping instead of helping."

"That's hardly a fair indictment when you decided to do all this when I wasn't around." Max frowned, zipping and unzipping her parka, a nervous habit developed from years waiting for the ski-tow. "You didn't see anyone on site last night, did you?"

"No, why?"

Max shrugged. "No reason." It wasn't Sloane's business if there were poachers in the woods, it was her own. "I just thought that if you're so desperate to stay up all night, maybe you can tell Mr. Parker that in addition to being the decorator, you could also be security."

"Max—" Orren started in a warning tone.

"Don't worry, I'm going," Max interrupted. "I'd hate to gatecrash the princess' beautifully couture landscape for luring in all the big fish investors."

"I'm trying to help, all you're doing is being negative," Sloane shot back. "For someone with her head so far up her own ass, I at least manage to get things done."

"You managed to wheedle your way into this job, one thing is for sure." Max smirked. "What's the matter, princess? No other lodges would take you, once you dropped out of qualifiers?"

Orren turned to face Max, his face stern and stony. "Enough, Carter. Take your petty bullshit off-site."

"She started it."

"I'm not so sure about that."

"Whatever," Max snapped, turning on the heel of her boot. "I'm gone."

Chapter 8

The slopes were empty, and Sloane's clients had canceled with intent to reschedule once the snow arrived. *If* it arrived, at that rate, with the sun beating down overhead so warm that she'd stripped down to a hoodie, leaving her parka back in her cabin. She kicked at the grass and the mud, frowning as it became caked into her boots.

"You ready?" Bev asked, jingling her car keys. "I can't be gone long. We might be light on guests, but I have to make something to impress those investors, and you know how people like that can be."

"Like what?" Sloane asked, and flinched at the defensiveness in her tone.

"You know. Picky. Rude. Entitled as all hell, sometimes."

"Not everyone is like that, you know."

Bev raised a skeptical eyebrow at her as she unlocked the car and climbed into the driver's seat. "I didn't say everyone was, I'm only talking about investors."

"I'm sorry, I just—it's been a long day already."

"I can imagine. I saw the main hall, it looks fantastic."

Sloane buckled her seat belt, her hands pressed down into the denim of her jeans, tactile and pleasantly distracting from the anxiety that prickled beneath her skin. "Thank you," she said, looking out the window at the valley below. "I didn't mind doing it."

"That makes one of us. Usually we all end up drawing straws to see who gets stuck with it. Looks like this year we didn't need to."

"It was something to do, I guess."

"Sure." Bev coasted her car down the slope, rotating her left shoulder with a pained expression on her face. "Damn, I wish contractors could still stay on-site. Getting up this early in the morning to drag my ass up the mountain is starting to take a toll on my beauty sleep."

"Why aren't you allowed to anymore?"

Bev shrugged. "Cuts. Always cuts, it never ends. Nothing ever expands in jobs like these, it only contracts, getting smaller and smaller until you're sure you might suffocate if you have to endure one more shift."

"Would you stay, if they asked you to?"

"Probably not, at this point. This place is beautiful, and I enjoy the work, but damn, they make it hard to want to keep showing up. Some days, I want to roll over and ignore all of it. Ignore the alarm, ignore the inevitable calls from Orren wondering where the hell I am, ignore getting fired when I don't pick up the phone. But I stay, because there are bills to pay, and people who depend on me, and that's more important than the rest of it."

"Heavy," Sloane said, pulling at a loose thread in her hoodie. "It's a shame so few of us have any real viable options to live life."

"We can't all be you, born with silver spoon in mouth," Bev replied, turning onto the road that led into town. Unlike the rough trail that led to the lodge, the pavement here was smooth and unblemished. "Some of us are born starving, and have to fight from the first breath."

"It comes with strings."

"What comes with strings?"

Sloane exhaled a sigh. "The silver spoon. The money, opportunities, all of it is a pathway to maintaining your family's credentials. You asked me earlier if I ever thought about doing something else, and the answer was no, will always be no, because I'm not allowed to choose anything else. Failure isn't an option."

"You're a grown-ass woman, Sloane."

"It's complicated."

"It's only complicated because you're afraid to give all that up." Bev stopped at an intersection and glanced at her before continuing. "You have the choice to turn your back on all of it, start over, begin again. Yeah, it's hard, but I'd rather live through hard than wind up on my deathbed with nothing more than regrets to keep me company."

"Are you always this intense?"

"If you don't want my advice, then fine. But you walk around the lodge looking like a ghost half the time, and the other half you're putting on the mask your parents made you. It's no way to live, not if you ask me." Bev sucked her teeth and frowned. "Honestly, I got to a point where I couldn't do it anymore. The fundraisers, the galas, the whispers, the rumors, the gossip, by the time I left I was ready to burn the whole place down in my wake."

"And did you?"

Bev sighed. "No. Like you said, it's complicated."

They rode in silence for much of the journey, accompanied by the low grumble of the engine and the shake of the car when it crossed over occasional potholes. Sun beat down, and even in just a hoodie, Sloane started to sweat, feeling it prickle at her forehead and under her arms.

"Almost there," Bev announced, nodding towards the town limits sign. "Few more minutes."

"Thank you again for agreeing to give me a ride."

"It must not be very nice, being all the way out here without a car."

Sloane drummed her fingertips against her knees. "I was hired last minute, I didn't have the time to drive if I was going to get to Crimson Oak on time."

"Still, it's not like buses run regularly up here. Not out this far, anyway."

"Yeah, they weren't very clear on that when they sent the paperwork over." Sloane tapped her thumb against her kneecap, savoring the quiet pops with each strike. "But it's not like I had many options, so who am I to complain?"

"Who hired you?"

"Mr. Parker."

Bev rolled her eyes as she pulled into a small parking lot. "Figures. He's always been like that. Talks a big game, rarely follows up on promises. Hell, I'm almost surprised that you haven't left the site in a huff already. I might have, if I were you."

"I might be spoiled, but I'm also stubborn."

"I never called you spoiled."

"No," Sloane replied, unbuckling her seatbelt as the car came to a stop.

"But you didn't have to, it's written all over your face. It's not unfamiliar."

"Alright," Bev said, and didn't argue. "Twenty minutes enough? Not much to do here, just the shop and the gas station unless you go further into town."

"Plenty."

"I'll stay out of your hair."

Sloane headed into the grocery store, while Bev wandered across to the gas station. The town was sparse there, just a few buildings, but more rose up out of the horizon in the distance, all brick and kitsch in that cutesy way that Sloane had always loved. There was something so cozy about a house with too much in it, or too many decorations, too many lights, too much sparkle. It was an innocent excess born of enthusiasm and joy, and there wasn't much of either left in the world.

The store was chilly and brightly lit, the icy draft wafting from the freezer section up towards the registers. Sloane took a basket and returned to the fish counter for the second time in two days. She hadn't anticipated a damned wolf taking off with two days' worth of a cache.

"Uh, hi," she said, calling over the glass panes. "I'd like some salmon, please."

"Oh, it's you again."

"Catering supply ran dry." An easy excuse, one no one would question. "You know how it is."

"Yep. How much this time?"

"Eight pounds."

"I don't know if I have that much. You almost cleaned me out yesterday."

"Whatever you've got, then, and substitute something else to make up the difference." She grimaced at the whiskers inside the case. "Just as long as it's not catfish."

"Freshly caught off the lake this morning. It's good stuff."

"It tastes like the dirt it lives in."

The fishmonger gave her a strange look before shrugging and beginning to pull whole fish from the case, piling them atop white paper until the scale read eight pounds. "That all?"

"Yes, thanks." Sloane glanced towards the front of the store, out the window to Bev's truck. "Can you triple wrap that? My, uh—friend—doesn't really like the smell of seafood."

"Then your friend doesn't know what they're missing. But sure."

She waited, taking the pack when it was ready and depositing it into her basket. She collected a few snacks for the next day, along with some juice, so that she hopefully wouldn't look as hungover and half-dead as she had that morning. If she continued to almost vomit in the kitchen, Bev really would think she was pregnant.

And she'd probably tell someone, and it would get out, and the rumor mill would spin into overdrive. All of her teammates back in Colorado would hear, and send tentative messages trying to tease what they thought was the truth out of her, just to whisper it back to whoever else, and on and on it would go. Her parents would hear, and they'd freak out, saying she'd thrown her career away, as if it wasn't already hanging on by a thread.

She was tired.

So pressingly, unbelievably, inescapably tired of all of it.

Most days she daydreamed of getting on a plane to anywhere, just to get away, to pretend at a new start, despite knowing that in three days she'd wind up on a return flight, because she'd never been strong enough to really take that leap.

"Thanks," she said, handing over a stack of bills to the cashier.

"Did you need a bag?"

"Uh, yeah." Sloane wrapped the fish again, this time in a plastic bag, already cursing herself internally for forgetting the reusable one back in her cabin. The guilt hissed in her lungs, not heavy, but persistent, and one breath in millions of others just like it. Thousands of tiny grievances against herself, inhaled deeply until the fiberglass of it shredded her from the inside out. "Thanks again."

Bev was already waiting by the car, leaning against it as though it was spring, and not winter, running a hand through her blond curls. "You ready?" she called over the empty parking lot.

"Yeah, I'm ready."

"Did they have what you were looking for?" Bev eyed the bag with interest, but didn't inquire.

"Yes." Sloane opened the passenger side door. "It's not a pregnancy test."

"I didn't ask."

"You didn't have to."

"Am I really that transparent?" Bev asked with a laugh.

"It's not a bad thing. It's actually kind of nice. Too many people speak in riddles, you know? Just tell me what you mean, so I can formulate a response."

"If you want bold, brash, and brutally honest, I'm your woman." Bev climbed in, slamming the door. "And if I'm being brutally honest, you seem pretty miserable."

"Wow."

"You said you wanted honesty, right?"

"Sure, but that's very—" Sloane sat back in the seat, looking over at her. "It's very forward."

"I'm that, too."

"I guess I am miserable, but who wouldn't be after losing out on the only thing you've been working towards for years?"

"Nah, it's a different kind of misery." Bev started the car and pulled out onto the road, letting the silence stand for a long moment. "Sorry, I shouldn't press."

"It's alright."

"Heartbreak?"

"I thought you said you shouldn't press?" Sloane said, almost laughing.

Bev flashed her a guilty look. "I'm sorry, I can't help it, I'm compelled by my own curiosity."

"Not a heartbreak. It's been a long time since that's been the case."

"How long?"

"Ten years."

"Hell of a dry spell for someone who looks like you."

Sloane snorted. "I didn't say dry spell, I said heartbreak. It's hard to find people in those hyper competitive circles, everyone wants to outdo everyone else, it's all a mess."

"Sounds like the corporate world, too."

"Probably."

"So who was the last one to break your heart?" Bev asked, her eyes fixed on the road. "You must have been young, what, early twenties?"

"Yeah." Sloane nodded, more to herself than to Bev. "She was in most of my classes at college. We were together for a few semesters, and then she moved out to the west coast."

"You didn't follow her?"

"She didn't want me to."

"Ouch." Bev glanced at her, throwing a sympathetic look in her direction. "What about Max, then?"

"What about her?"

"Well, you know, you're both..." Bev trailed off, wobbling her head from side to side. "You know."

"Gay? Lesbians?"

"Yeah."

"I didn't actually know that about her, but I suppose I should have guessed." Sloane sighed, leaning her head against the glass of the window. "I'm pretty sure we hate each other, actually."

"There's a fine line between—"

"Not so fine, actually, in situations like these, Bev."

"Fair enough."

Gravel rattled beneath the tires over a rough patch of road, a patchwork of repairs that had been done over a long period of time, newer sections deep tar black, and the older, faded, pocked, and riddled with fissures. Sloane watched each tree as they drove past, observing them in the side mirror as they grew smaller and faded into the distance like so much else, until they were nothing more than dots on the horizon. "It's beautiful out here," she said finally, when she'd closed the old tome in her mind that was filled with eighteen months of forbidden memories. "I wish I could stay longer."

"More beautiful than Colorado?"

"Just beautiful in a different way, I guess."

Bev nodded, turning onto the small road that led to the lodge. "I'd love to make it out there one day. If not to live, then maybe to visit."

"The slopes there are amazing."

"Despite working at a winter sports lodge, I don't participate in that myself. I'm more of a rock climber than someone who wants to artfully and speedily slide down them."

"I've never been rock climbing."

"You should try it. In fact, there's a place a couple of hours from here, if you want to see how well your skills translate."

Sloane laughed. "Not well, I'm imagining."

"You'd be surprised."

"How about your husband, does he rock climb too?"

"Nah," Bev answered, shaking her head as yellowing grass shone golden in the afternoon light. "My kids don't either, but I don't mind. It's some time on my own, to get my head on straight. To remember what's important in life, to gain a little perspective at the top of the wall, even for a few seconds before you rappel back down."

"You're full of life lessons today."

"Sorry. I've just been where you are, or where I think you might be, and I'd hate it if you wasted another ten years like I did."

"I don't believe in wasted time. Every moment we exist is one we're learning from, even if it's the wrong lessons initially. It's all part of it."

Bev parked the car, taking the keys from the ignition. "I'll be heading back to town in a few days, if you want a ride."

"Thanks. I'll let you know, but unless we get some snow up here fast, I can't imagine that I'll be particularly busy."

"Lucky you. I'll be draining away my life force in the kitchen, cooking for people who earn my entire year's earnings in the time it takes them to send food back to the kitchen."

Sloane unbuckled herself, taking the bag with her. "Don't drain yourself too much, everyone else still needs to be fed."

"Pff," Bev replied with a puff of air at her lips. "Try telling them that."

Chapter 9

Max padded through the woods, grateful to be shifted. The pinpricks of it lived beneath her skin during a full moon, even when it was broad daylight. The bone-tired ache was soothed by the Wolf within her, but she knew that by the time morning arrived, she'd feel like warmed-up roadkill.

What was left of the snow was quickly turning to slush, even that high up the mountain. She frowned, or would have had she been human, and it came out as a stunted growl instead. Something about the forest felt off, something wasn't right. Poachers, maybe, or something else, it was hard to discern as a Wolf when there was no scent to help her. Whoever had been up on the mountain had been using something to mask their scent.

She shook her head, fur jostling gently from side to side in the gentle breeze. She can't have seen a bear, that was absurd. Some weren't unheard of in the area, but those were black bears, much smaller, and more importantly, not white. It must have been a trick of the light, or, more likely, someone had dosed the salmon she'd eaten, maybe with tranquilizers that hadn't metabolized correctly. As a Wolf, she metabolized medicines, poisons, and toxins much faster than in her human form.

Something on the breeze pulled her attention, and she lifted her snout to the air, sniffing diligently. Fish. Frustration burned in her gut, and she set off on a mission to find it, to throw the entire lot of it off the cliff-face, and given the opportunity, tear some poachers limb from limb. Guns didn't scare her, they never had, because they were always terrified of her, all thumbs and stumbling over their feet in their desperation to get away.

It was almost uncomfortably warm at the summit, even standing headlong in the wind. Looking out over the nightscape, she almost expected to see bluebonnets peeking out from beneath the fading blanket of white, but found only desperate grass and the crushing oblivion of ten thousand unrealized dreams. Whatever life was, it wasn't fair, and it chewed at her insides, day in, and day out, knowing that her life was held in the balance between two warring factions within her.

Max had realized early on that she was never going to go pro. For that you needed money, and sponsors, and free rent while you built it all up, and she had none of those things. Neither did her family. She spent years working minimum-wage retail just to try to make ends meet, just to come up to Crimson Oak for a few months each year and feel like more of a person than she ever did folding jeans at the local chain store.

No one ever respected her. Not there. Not in any of the places where she showed up for work just to be berated about not doing enough, not meeting targets, not signing up enough people for the store's predatory credit card during every shift.

But on the mountain, she was knowledgeable, she was strong, and certain, and sure of herself, and if she could hide out in those woods year-round and not starve, she'd do it with a smile. Protecting Bear Mountain felt like a mission worth having, and one she felt capable enough to accomplish.

The smell of fish wafted on the gentle breeze, and she padded through the mud, feeling it squish up through the pads of her paws and loving every moment of it. Tactile and enticing, despite knowing she'd look like she'd been dragged backwards through a hedge the next morning. It was salmon again, but something else this time, too. Another fish, maybe, she didn't eat much seafood in her human form. Too expensive, despite loving it.

It didn't take her long to find the first cache of fish, hung from a low-hanging tree branch, just out of her reach. Max circled beneath it, judging the distance, working the problem, her mind just slightly fuzzy at the edges in her Wolf form. Shifted, she was more raw emotion and impulse than coherent thought, but there was an honesty to it that most people would find threatening if a human behaved that way. She jumped once, twice, but was only able to brush against the bottom of the burlap bag.

Wary, she sat back on her haunches for a moment, listening for the sounds of snapped twigs, or footsteps squelching on the wet ground, but heard neither. There was no scent around the cache, either, nothing beyond the smell of fish. The poachers from before had always smelled of doe estrus, but there was no sign of that, no hint as to who'd left it there or why. It had to be poachers, there was no other explanation. Why else would someone be leaving what was probably fifty dollars worth of fish hanging from a tree branch at least a mile off the trail?

Satisfied that no one was watching her, lining up a shot, she jumped again, snapping her jaws, this time snagging on the burlap. Planks of salmon and tilapia tumbled out, and her stomach growled greedily. It almost hurt her physically to nose the fish, one at a time, over the edge of the nearby cliff face. If the previous cache had been laced with something, it was almost certain that this one was, too. All that fish, wasted, and for what? So some poacher could mount a taxidermied wolf in his house? They were endangered, and no one should be hunting them.

She was the only Wolf in the area, so far as she could tell, and that had been true for years. There used to be another in the local town when she first started working at Crimson Oak, but he'd disappeared one day, upped sticks and moved out to Montana for work. And, as far as she could tell, there were no wolves on Bear Mountain, either. Not anymore. Not after the last set of poachers she hadn't been quick enough to dispatch.

The cache emptied, she lifted her snout to the wind, hunting for the next. That wasn't all of it, the enticing scent of salmon still hung on the breeze.

Max huffed out a sigh into the night air, a shooting star catching her eyes in the moonlit sky. So impossibly far away, and yet, something that felt primal within her. How many Wolves, how many humans had stared up at the shifting stars, season after season, century after century, lost in wonderment? It was as natural and necessary as breathing, but so many had forgotten to remember to look up and realize their place in the universe—infinitesimally small, but indispensable.

The second cache was near the bank of the narrow river that cut through the side of the mountain, treacherous in the spring with its rushing waters, now tamed to a lazy trickle with the lack of snow. It was half buried, with a large hollow log covering part of it. Grunting, she dug furiously, mud flying through moonbeams and starlight, splattering across her muzzle until she grasped the sack, yanking it from the earth.

More salmon, more tilapia. Whoever these poachers were, they had money to burn if they were offering up the choicest of cuts, and not the usual fish heads and deer intestines. She dragged the sack to the water, tossing it in. Even in the slow current, the sack washed away downstream, a little at a time, and it burned in her gut that someone would waste good food like that when so many were going hungry even in the local town. It was the height of selfishness, of posturing wealth, and it all told quite a story about who was out here trying to bag themselves a trophy kill.

Her stomach growled again, and she wandered through the woods, slowly heading back to her little enclave that she'd built for herself years ago out there on the mountain. It was no more than a natural lean-to, nothing that would look particularly out of place to the untrained eye. Half of a shed in size, built out of naturally fallen logs and halfway thatched with pine boughs that she replaced every season. She curled up on the blanket she'd left for herself there, tucking into the basket of chicken she'd pilfered from the kitchen earlier. There were certain benefits to being someone who'd worked there for years, and one of them was having a copy of the key. Bev had never even mentioned the missing food, not in years of it happening. Maybe she hadn't noticed, or maybe she assumed Orren was having one hell of a midnight snack.

The chicken was cooked, despite her Wolfish stomach craving the slimy satisfaction of raw chicken, but it had only taken one bout with salmonella after shifting back too soon to change her mind on the matter. The Wolf may crave raw meat, but Max preferred the safety of rotisserie chicken, tearing strips off of it and barely chewing before swallowing it down, part of her angry and frustrated at the lack of gore. It was a Wolf thing, and probably the part she liked least.

Licking her chops, she yawned, nudging aside the empty parcel. It wasn't far from dawn, and soon, the sky would be shot through with spikes of pinks and oranges, a preview of daylight, almost unwelcome if it weren't for her keen desire to crawl back into bed, something she couldn't do as a Wolf, not without alarming Bev, Orren, any guests that might still be on site, and Sloane. Though, given her attitude, Max wouldn't mind scaring her. Maybe it would be the reality check she needed to stop being so annoying.

Ski instructors were usually full of themselves, at least, the ones that Mr. Parker hired always were, lording it over all the snowboarders, acting like they owned the slopes. She was tired of it, so bone tired of leaving one job where she was dismissed and disregarded just to have someone try to do the same up there at Crimson Oak. Max never let them do that, of course, but they all certainly did try.

The way she'd showed up the previous year's ski instructor was probably why he hadn't come back. He'd challenged her, and she'd won easily, and he'd stomped off back to his cabin and spent the final six weeks of the season sulking, refusing to even acknowledge her presence. It had been a nice, peaceful existence without him constantly butting in, and she hoped to repeat the experience with Sloane.

People like her didn't understand, could never understand what life was like for normal people. For people who always had to check the bank balance before grocery shopping, who spent weeks fretting about a necessary forty-dollar purchase, who spent more time with their bank balance in the red than out of it. People like Sloane Hearst had never gone to bed hungry, or skipped a field trip because they couldn't afford it, or sat shivering in their house because the heat was too expensive. They all thought that they worked harder than anyone else, and everyone struggling had simply chosen to live that way.

The inequality of it was a constant ember in her chest, ready to flare at the first provocation. Back home, a few hours south, she swallowed that impulse for ten months of the year. Up on Bear Mountain, the one place she knew better than anyone else, even Mr. Parker, she couldn't. It stuck in her throat and threatened to strangle her, cutting off her access to air until she fought it back with snide remarks, or challenges, or whatever they needed to get off her back and let her do her job.

Max circled, trying to get comfortable, but couldn't. Her muscles were too coiled beneath her fur, the adrenaline from finding the caches not yet spent.

Stretching her front legs out in front of her, she bent into a deep bow before readying herself to run.

She sprinted through the woods, paws deep in mud, like running through quicksand, and the fatigue of it burned in her shoulders but she allowed it to settle there, even knowing she'd be sore as hell as soon as she shifted back. The mountain was empty, and there was only her, and the moon overhead, calling out for her howl. It was what she spent ten months yearning for, the thick scent of fresh pine, the trees cast in their bluish glow, and at least there, she had the space to run in a way she didn't back home. Suburbs didn't like forest preserves, when they could be made into shopping centers, instead.

Her muscles ached, but she relished it despite her exhaustion. She'd only have one more shift to Wolf on Bear Mountain if the snowboarding program got cut to impress the investors, and even the half-conscious thought of that stopped her dead in her tracks. No more Crimson Oak, no more boarding, no more winters spent in her little cabin, no more escaping from the sickeningly dull treachery of constantly rotating shifts, thirty-nine hours a week, nothing more than cheap noodles to look forward to as she tried to scrape together some kind of living and failed at it, month after month. It dragged at her, threatening to pull her under, to drown her in the incessant inevitability of it.

People like her rarely broke through to anything else. Education had long since priced her out, and when she was young, she'd been too busy trying to pay her family's rent to go, anyway. The reminder that Crimson Oak might soon be as inaccessible as taking up yachting as a hobby tore something inside her, and she slumped against a tree, letting the bark push past dense fur into skin. Had she been Max, and not Wolf, she would have cried.

Instead, she howled.

A deep echo across the distant valley, rustling through pine needles and empty deciduous branches, past the trickling river, settling somewhere dark and hopeless for just a moment before the ember caught fire in her lungs again and she knew she'd have to fight for it, just like she had everything else. Nothing she had was gained without the endless battle to obtain it, and though it was unjust and unfair, it had taught her how to scrap and scream and pull what she needed from life, one hell-bent guttural cry after the next.

Max steadied herself, pushing away from the trunk of the huge pine, and began to run again, as if she could outrun the struggles that life still had in store for her.

Chapter 10

Sloane staggered out of the woods as soon as she shifted back to her human form, weak from hunger and ravenous. Bev wouldn't be in for hours, as the investors never got up particularly early, and had complained about the timing of breakfast the day before. If she could drive, she'd head into town, but she'd flown out to Crimson Oak, and her car was back in Colorado, sitting useless in her parents' driveway.

Damned wolves. She thought she'd hidden the caches well enough, but once again, they'd beaten her to them. She was especially surprised that the tree cache had been emptied, and was still cursing herself for not raising it just five more inches off the ground, even hours after she'd discovered the limp burlap.

She hadn't expected there to be wolves on Bear Mountain, at least, not so many, and not so smart, either. Hunger ached in her gut and static fuzzed at the corners of her vision. It was like having the flu, if the flu came around every month just to knock you off your game, ruin your scoring, make it so that your every waking thought was food, and not being able to sleep off the shift the next day made for a punishing daily rhythm.

The door to the kitchen was locked, just as she knew it would be, and probably for the best. If she got in there, she'd clear the place out, leaving no more than crumbs, and that would raise far too many questions, especially with almost no guests on site. No doubt the investors wouldn't be impressed with an empty breakfast buffet, and if they liked Crimson Oak enough, they might be persuaded to keep both programs, at least for a couple more years while they worked on plans to reinvigorate the place. Breakfasts weren't enough on their own, but they certainly helped.

Sloane dragged herself back to her cabin, throwing herself on the bed, sticks, mud, and all. She barely had the energy to unwrap a few protein bars and choke them down, roiling angrily in her stomach. It wasn't enough, but it would have to do, and so she laid there, willing them to digest, to curb the gnawing hunger inside of her, at least enough that she wouldn't look half-rabid when Bev did show up in a few hours, busting through the kitchen door like a wild animal.

Another protein bar down, and she groaned. The taste of them was unpleasantly chalky and deeply unpleasant, the saccharine imitation chocolate taste coating her tongue, unavoidable and upsettingly present in her mouth. She lay back, allowing sleep to overtake her, if only for a few hours.

* * *

"Ms. Hearst?" a voice called through the door to her cabin.

Sloane opened one eye and groaned. "Mr. Ralt?"

"I'm sorry to bother you, but Mr. Parker wanted to see you."

"Me? Why?"

"I'm not sure, but he's in a meeting with the investors."

Her stomach growled audibly. "Do I have time to stop by the kitchen?"

"I'm afraid not. It's after ten."

She jumped out of the bed, her head reeling, stumbling over the frame. "Sorry, I think I slept through my alarm," she called through the door, tugging on a Crimson Oak polo shirt and jeans, followed by thick socks and hiking boots. "That doesn't usually happen to me."

"It's alright, happens to the best of us," he said, though there was a quiet tone of impatience to his words.

Sloane threw open the door with what she hoped was an open, professional smile, but the surprise and dismay that flashed across his face told her otherwise. "Sir?"

"Did you go for a hike last night?"

"Uh—"

"You have sticks in your hair, Ms. Hearst."

Feeling heat explode across her face and neck, she closed the door on him without thinking. "I, uh—sorry, Mr. Ralt, I'll just be a minute, I'll, uh—"

"I don't recommend hiking at night, Ms. Hearst, especially if you don't know the mountain."

"I get around well enough," she replied, almost gasping at her reflection. It wasn't just the sticks in her hair, it was the mud caked into her elbows, and the shallow scratches across her nose and cheeks from the brambles she'd gotten tangled in while looking for her pilfered food. No wonder he didn't recommend she hike at night, it looked like she'd had a rough time of it. "I enjoy the challenge of unfamiliar terrain."

"That may be so, but there are likely poachers on the mountain."

She stopped brushing her hair halfway down the strands, frozen in the mirror. "Poachers?"

"It's happened before, about five years back. Hunters trying for wolf trophies. They aren't supposed to be up this way, but with so few staff members, it's hard to keep tabs on."

"Poachers," she said again, quieter this time. She finished pulling the brush through her hair, sending several twigs and what looked like half a tree's worth of pine needles to the floor in a delicate rain of foliage. "What will Mr. Parker do about it?"

"Not much he can do if he doesn't catch them in the act. He won't hire security, there's too much open land up here to patrol effectively." He drummed his fingers against the door, probably not meaning to rush her, but it had the same effect.

Sloane glanced at the open door with a grimace. "I'm almost done," she apologized, scrubbing the mud from her elbows. No doubt her knees looked the same, but at least they were covered by her jeans. She stepped to the door, trying for another winning smile, but he only tilted his head at her.

"Are you alright, Ms. Hearst?"

"Sure, why wouldn't I be?"

"You look a little peaky." He raised an eyebrow. "Bev said that you didn't look well yesterday, either."

"I'm not pregnant."

"I didn't say that."

"Bev did." Sloane closed the door behind her and locked it. "But I'm not, and I'm fine. Just a little groggy, I don't usually sleep through my alarm."

"If you say so."

"I'm fine," she reiterated, hearing her tone grow sharper as the words passed over her lips. "Where is the meeting?"

"Behind the main hall. The investors couldn't resist what they're calling wonderful weather."

Sloane frowned. This kind of weather will ruin a place like this. It will drive down profits, it will—"

"I think their emphasis on the matter is probably the point," he said sadly. "Push the price down, rip this place apart, start fresh. It's only a matter of time, now, before Crimson Oak ceases to exist the way it once did."

"I'm just sorry I've never been here before now."

"I didn't think you'd enjoy a place like this, not after some of the resorts you've trained at."

"Frankly, Mr. Ralt, I am tired of training."

"I'm sorry to hear that."

"It is what it is." She rolled her shoulder in its socket, wincing at the pain. "Are you coming to this meeting, too?"

"Just you, I'm afraid. I don't tend to do well in high-pressure situations like this. I stumble over my words and I'm pretty useless. I might be fantastic at running this lodge, but I'm a liability where investors are concerned, and Mr. Parker knows it."

"I still don't know why they want to see me, of all people. I've barely even been here a week."

"Just go with it, Ms. Hearst."

"You can call me Sloane, you know. Ms. Hearst sounds so formal." She glanced at him from the corner of her eye. "Unless you prefer that formality, Mr. Ralt."

"Orren."

"Orren," she repeated with a smile. "Here I go, then." Her hand rested on the brass handle for a moment before pulling it open. "Wish me luck."

"Don't sell us out," he said, his stare boring into her. "I know you're new here, but this is a special place, and—"

Sloane nodded. "I know. I'll do my best, whatever that looks like." She stepped over the threshold, slightly irritated at how washed out and cluttered the decorations looked in the natural morning light. They were far more impressive at night, when the lights sparkled across the room, dangling from the ceiling like icicles. In the warm glow of sunlight, though, the delicate snowflakes looked more like a child's art project. She frowned at them, already calculating how to improve them, how to make the place really glitter with potential, even at eleven in the morning.

The rich scent of coffee wafted through the main hall, and it turned her stomach. The protein bars sat in her gut like lead, weighing her down without granting her even one iota of the energy they'd promised. "Gentlemen," she said, easing open the door to the rear garden. "I was told you wanted to see me?"

"Ah, Ms. Hearst, please sit down," Mr. Parker gestured. He looked the way men like him always did, pristine, unused parka, subtle designer jeans, and boots with a price tag so high, even Sloane would never touch that brand. He nodded with an encouraging smile. "Thank you for joining us on such short notice. As I understand it you've been quite busy since you arrived, despite the lack of snow." He shot her a warning look before covering it with an empty smile.

"Er—yes, of course," she lied. "Very busy. Barely a moment to call my own, in fact."

"How are you finding Crimson Oak?" one of the investors asked, a tall, hulking man who barely fit into the chair he was sitting in. His voice was intimidatingly deep, and she took a step back out of instinct.

"It's a wonderful resort," she parroted from what Mr. Parker had told her in her brief interview, more for show than a test of her skill. "It's unmatched in personality and beauty."

The investor laughed. "How long did you prep her before this meeting, Parker?" he asked, folding his hands atop the glass table, lit from below with stranded lights, the glow barely visible in the bright daylight. "Ms. Hearst, if you please, your honest opinion about Crimson Oak."

"It has endless potential. The slopes here are well maintained, and the proximity to the regional airport makes it easily accessible."

"And what about the fact that over ninety percent of guests at Crimson Oak last year were locals to the general area?"

Sloane blinked, trying to resist the urge to fidget. "I wouldn't know, this is my first year here."

"Our concerns," he continued, gesturing at the rest of the men around the table, "are that this place won't be capable of drumming up enough business, not with this location, and while we would prefer to focus on team-building retreats here, were we to purchase this location, we feel that most corporations looking for a place to go would choose somewhere like Aspen."

"Aspen is very nice, yes," she agreed. "I've spent a lot of time there over the years."

"How does Crimson Oak compare to some of the lodges in Aspen?" he asked, pen poised over a yellow legal pad of paper.

"It's... rustic, to be sure," she stammered. "But with the right investment—"

"Our organization—SyndiCorp, that is—well, we would hope to start recouping our investment almost immediately. With the markets being what they are, all the volatility makes some of our shareholders nervous, you understand."

"I mean, sure, I understand that, but—"

"If we were to purchase Crimson Oak by the end of the season, how soon do you think this place would turn a profit?"

Sloane's palms were sweating, her mouth dry with her tongue laying limply against her jaw like a recalcitrant slug. "I'm not familiar with this lodge's finances, sir, nor am I someone who deals in management. I am a ski instructor."

"You are being far too modest, Ms. Hearst. We know your family ties, surely you have some insider knowledge about this place that you can share. Your family has been known in these circles for years, generations even, and your input would be greatly appreciated." He glanced down at the pad of paper, noting something in the margins that she couldn't quite make out from the other end of the table. He cleared his throat before continuing, "If you were to assist us in this matter, I can personally guarantee that you'd be considered a very valuable asset in our corporate offices out west."

Sloane chewed her lip for just a fraction of a moment too long, considering what he'd said. It could be a way out, a new path forward, an opportunity to start fresh and leave her embarrassing failures behind.

"Ms. Hearst would love to be of assistance, I'm sure," Mr. Parker interjected, shooting her a look. "She is a valued member of our team here at Crimson Oak, and we are more than lucky to have her. I'm sure she will do whatever she can to facilitate this deal moving forward." He stared, eyes narrowed. "Isn't that right, Ms. Hearst?"

"Yes, of course," she replied, finally finding her voice. "Whatever I can." She wasn't entirely sure what she could really offer them beyond quiet suggestions of improvements, but with their desperation to turn a profit, any hope of real investment was coasting steadily downhill.

"Excellent," the investor said, beaming. He held out his hand to her and gave her a firm, intentionally intimidating shake. "Here's my card. Please feel free to call if you have any thoughts. I know reception up here isn't the greatest, and being honest, that is one of our greatest concerns in the cost-profit analysis."

"Understood," Sloane said, taking the card. It was firm in her hands, embossed with the Syndicorp logo across the top. It read Mark Darius, chief investment officer in gold metallic lettering. Pompous but professional, just like most of her parents' friends—if you could even call them that. Most would throw their own mothers to the wolves if it earned them another half a percentage point in interest.

The investors all stood and left the rear garden, leaving her alone with Mr. Parker. She shifted nervously, putting the card into her back pocket. "I'm sorry if my lateness delayed things, I was unaware that I needed to be here," she said.

"Things were starting to go south, I thought your insight may help things along." He glanced up from his laptop and nodded. "And it did, at least, so far as I can tell."

"I'm not so sure I'm the best person to be in these meetings, sir, I don't have much experience in these arenas."

"You look the part, Ms. Hearst, and they trust your opinion."

"I look the part?"

Mr. Parker sighed. "You come from a good family. You know lodges, that much is true, and you've associated with people like these investors for years, no?"

"I guess, but that doesn't mean I've done it well. I'm not really one for public speaking or giving presentations."

"Are you saying that you won't assist this deal?"

Sloane took a step backwards, trying to steady herself against the wave of nausea roiling in her stomach. "No, I'm just saying that someone else on site may be better suited to giving information to your investors, someone who actually knows this place. I've only been here a week."

"I know that you're an athlete and a businesswoman, Ms. Hearst, but surely by now you realize that much of this is appearances, no?"

"I think Orren would be better suited to this."

"Orren has already made his objections to this deal crystal clear, and as such I cannot trust him to be in these meetings. He's been a wonderful manager of this place for years, but some people just can't handle change, they spit on progress. Things have to change, or this place isn't going to do anything other than rot into the ground."

Sloane shoved her hands into her pockets, trying to hide her fidgeting. "I don't have a mind for business. Meetings like these make me uncomfortable. As you said, I'm an athlete, not a business partner."

"And I've already told you why that doesn't matter. These investors, they want to see people who look like them, talk like them, went to the same kinds of schools as them. Where did you attend college, Ms. Hearst?"

"Dartmouth."

"There, you see? Two of the investors at this table today also attended Dartmouth. They will see you as the voice of reason, as someone who skis as often as she can and knows what kinds of amenities people in your circles are looking for."

"Surely some of them are skiers, too."

"Occasional skiers, but no one of your caliber."

"I'm not sure if I even have a caliber anymore," she mumbled. "Not after missing the qualifiers."

"Your name still carries weight. Your last name more so than your first, if you catch my drift. Long after your skiing days are over, you will hold influence in the winter sporting community by nature of your name and education alone."

"Sir—"

"Ms. Hearst, I know you probably wondered why we brought you out here, and this is why. Your skiing credentials are a drop in the pond compared to what your name can bring this negotiation." He closed his laptop and gestured to the chair across from him. "Please sit down, we have a number of things to discuss, including the arrival of a few more members of their team."

Chapter 11

When Max opened her cabin door, she hadn't expected to see Sloane standing on the wooden steps, her bags and skis in hand. Max held the door firm, her eyes narrowed. "What do you want?"

"Let me in, we're bunking together."

"The hell we are."

"Take it up with Mr. Parker if you must, this wasn't my idea." Sloane dropped her bags on the stoop, shrugging theatrically at her. "They have more investors coming in this afternoon."

"Then they can stay in the lodge, it's not like there isn't plenty of room in there with this weather chasing everyone else away."

"They want to try out the cabins because they may be turned into private accommodations when this place gets bought out."

Max snorted. "*When?* I thought we were still thinking *if.*"

"Not judging by what I just saw. They want the cabins to serve as penthouses for the CEOs."

"The staff cabins? These are hardly up to the kinds of standards those old windbags would want."

"Yes, that's why they're having a few from their research and development team stay there, to make notes on what would need updating, and how they could do so efficiently." Sloane laid a hand on her hip. "Are you going to let me in, or what?"

"Or what. Tell Mr. Parker you'll be sleeping in the kitchen, then, because you're not coming in here. I've always had this cabin, ever since I started working here, and—"

"You want me to sleep on the kitchen floor?" Sloane asked with incredulity. "Fine." She smirked, her eyes narrowed. "I'll be sure to tell Mr. Parker that you're not exactly being a team player. I'm sure that it won't impact who stays after mid-season."

Max growled loudly, pushing the door open. "Fine. But don't touch anything."

"I wouldn't dare, I might catch something."

"Yeah, like a clue."

"You're the one who needs to catch a clue, Carter, this place is changing one way or another, whether you like it or not, no matter what objections you and Orren might have. These investors have the cash, and the motivation, and it's very obvious that Mr. Parker is trying to sell up and get out of this business before he winds up bankrupt."

"He's far from bankrupt."

"I'm not so sure about that. It doesn't take long for a place like this to pull you under, the running costs are astronomical."

"Not with what they're paying us."

"Insurance, Carter, the insurance is more expensive than you can even imagine."

"I can imagine plenty, thank you very much." Max gestured to the top bunk of the bed. "That one is yours, I've already claimed bottom."

"I hate the top bunk, I'm always afraid it's going to break."

"Not my problem."

"What *is* your problem?"

Max rolled her eyes, making sure Sloane saw it. "*You* are my problem, obviously. You and every other entitled yahoo out on this mountain, thinking they can do whatever they like with no consequences."

"I haven't done anything out of the ordinary."

"No, you're right about that, I've come to expect garbage attitudes like yours from ski instructors. It's as obvious and unavoidable as air."

"Your attitude isn't much better, I'll have you know. You've been gunning for me since the moment I arrived in reception. You took one look at me and decided that was it, you were going to hate me on sight."

"Please, it's not hard to tell who you are. Brand new, top of the line gear, cover shoots with Winter Sports Magazine, and ivy-league education, oh yeah, Hearst, I managed to look you up when I was down the mountain. You're everything I've come to expect."

"You're painting with awfully broad strokes, Carter. You don't know me at all."

Max snorted. "I know plenty."

"Alright, fine, let's play that game then, shall we?" Sloane dumped her bags on the floor, propping her skis up against the wall next to the snowboard. "You walk around with a perpetual chip on your shoulder, looking for fights where there aren't any because you have so much pent up aggression that you can barely function on a day to day basis. How's that for a read?"

"Please, you wouldn't last one shift in my shoes back home. You'd crumple ten minutes in."

"You were sure I'd crumple here, too, but I haven't left yet, have I?"

"It's different."

"Sure."

"I bet you've never worked a real job in your life, Hearst." Max tilted her chin, raising her eyebrows in challenge. "I bet you've had every damn thing in your life handed to you on a shining, polished silver platter, and you wouldn't know what hard work was if it stood up and punched you right in the middle of that pretty face you have."

"I've worked plenty, and training for nationals is hardly a walk in the park."

"It's more opportunity than most people will see in a lifetime."

"I worked hard for that opportunity."

"You were born with a silver spoon in your mouth and can't understand anyone who wasn't. I'm sure you got up early, I'm sure you trained until you vomited up chunks of your bougie chef-prepared breakfast, I'm sure you panicked every time a joint in your knee started acting up, but it's nothing on what most people endure day in, and day out. Hell, ask Bev what she has to deal with, I'm sure she'd be more than happy to tell you."

"Bev is the only person here who went out of their way to treat me like a person."

"That's because she's a good person, unlike some of us."

"You think I'm a bad person because of who my parents are?" Sloane asked, arms folded over her chest. "Seriously?"

"I think you're a bad person because you stormed in here like a hurricane, acting like you owned the damned place."

"I haven't even unpacked yet, what are you talking about?"

"Not the cabin, dork, Crimson Oak."

"Oh." Sloane uncrossed her arms, letting them drop to her sides. "You didn't make it easy, I've been on the defensive since day one. You decided I was going to be an ass, and that was that."

"I was right, though, you *are* an ass."

"Fine. Just stay out of my way."

"The closet and the wardrobe are full, you'll have to work out of your bags." Max glared at her and shrugged. "Anyone else would do the same in this situation."

"I don't care. Some of us are used to living out of suitcases, it's nothing new to me."

"Must be nice, having all your travel paid for."

"My travel isn't paid for," Sloane answered tersely. "But once again I see that you've already decided who I am, and nothing I do will have any impact one way or another on your opinion."

"I'll change my opinion when I'm proved wrong." Max sat on her bed, pulling on a pair of socks. "So far, I've had no need to change my stance."

"I'm going out to the slopes," Sloane announced, refusing to acknowledge Max's point. "I'll be back later."

"Good luck skiing on grass," Max taunted. "Haven't you seen what it looks like out there?"

"I could ski better on grass than you can board on snow."

"Prove it, princess."

Sloane rounded on her, pointing, jaw set firm. "I'm no princess. I'm tougher than you think I am, Carter."

"Is that a threat?"

"No, it's a warning to stay the hell away from me so long as we're both here."

"Whatever you say, princess." Max leaned back on her bed and yawned, feigning sleep. "You don't faze me."

"I—you know what, never mind." Sloane slammed the door in her wake, shaking the walls of the cabin so much that the map of the site, framed, fell behind the desk with the telltale crunch of glass.

"Figures," Max grumbled, turning onto her side. No space of her own, not at home, and not at Crimson Oak, always sharing rooms, and ceding space, and it was never ending and so tiresome that she wanted to scream into her pillow.

And then she did, and the muffled sound was so quiet that even that made her feel stifled. Sloane's bags on the floor, blocking the door from opening all the way, her stuff already an imposition. Max grumbled under her breath, shoving her feet into a pair of boots, despite the temperature. She hadn't anticipated a heat wave, so boots were all she had with her from home.

Locking the door behind her, she crossed the grounds, frowning at the state of the slopes, yellow-green with dying grass, with only delicate hints of snow still lingering in the shade of the forest. She pushed into reception and flopped into the chair, draping her legs over the arms.

"Orren," she complained, drawing out the final consonant.

"Max," he replied, not even bothering to look up from the newspaper. "Why do you sound like you're about to ruin my day?"

"Did you know that Parker was going to force us to share a cabin?"

"No, I did not."

"Something about the investors wanting to turn them into luxury accommodation, so they're taking most of the cabins over." She let her head drop backwards over the chair, almost savoring the painful stretch and strain in her neck. "I bet you didn't have to give yours up."

"I imagine they would have made me, were there any other men on site."

"I'd rather room with you than her."

"As fond as I am of you, I can't say the feeling is mutual."

She sat up straight, planting her feet on the ground. "What?"

"Some of us like to insulate ourselves against the kinds of roommates that would soak your mattress in freezing water just before bed."

"I'd never do that to you."

"Not until I got on your bad side, which judging by previous yearly calculations, happens about four times a day."

Max frowned, leaning forward to drain the coffee pot into a mug. "You've never been on my bad side. I give you a hard time, sure, but—"

"We're not here that long, can't you just stick it out until one of you is gone?" he asked, the heavy weight of it hanging perilously in the air. "Sorry," he mumbled, looking back down at the papers on his desk.

"Wow," Max said. "Thanks for that, Orren."

"You're losing your seasonal job. I'm losing everything if this deal gets messed up. If I tow the line, and keep my mouth shut, there's a pretty good possibility that they keep me on. If not, well, I'm out on my ass and quickly forgotten."

"I'd be here year-round if I could, but there's no budget!"

"I know you see Syndicorp taking over as a bad thing, but—"

Max barked out a laugh, interrupting him. "It is a bad thing, what makes you think there could be any other outcome?"

"Because despite all the cynicism you come in here and spew, I'm trying to keep my head above water with all of this. Times are changing, and people like you and I can't do much to stop it in its tracks. We can either swallow it down and make the best of it, or get shredded trying to fight the inevitable."

"I guess some of us would rather be shredded."

Orren sighed, rubbing at his left temple. "You're young yet."

"I'm almost thirty."

"Young," he reiterated. "I'm further down that road than you, and let me tell you, I've learned some hard lessons along the way. Painful ones." He sighed again. "Expensive ones."

"So what, your solution is to just give up?"

"You might call it that, I'm calling it going with the flow. Sometimes you just have to take the loss and try to make whatever you can out of it. There isn't always a third option, Max."

"Roll over and let them have whatever they want? That's your wise life advice?"

"My life advice is to stop throwing yourself at a brick wall and expecting that you're going to do more damage to it than it will do to you. My advice is to pick your battles, and try to make sure they're ones you can win."

Max pulled her knees to her chest, hands gripped around the mug. The coffee was too bitter and it was lukewarm, if that, but she sipped at it nonetheless. "So what are their plans for this place?"

"A focus on business retreats from what I understand. I don't know, it's hard to say before I've seen the plans." He glanced at the empty coffee pot and frowned. "And they aren't showing the likes of me the plans."

"They should, you know more than anyone." She sipped at the coffee, grimacing at the awful taste. "That reminds me, I found more bait caches on the mountain last night."

"More?"

"Yeah. Two this time, one hanging from a branch, the other buried under an old felled tree. My bet is that they were trying to keep me—er, trying to keep the animals they're baiting in one place long enough to line up a shot."

"Any other evidence?"

"No. Unfortunately."

Orren turned, marking a note on his calendar. "Twice in a week isn't a good sign. They're getting bolder."

"Bolder maybe, but not smarter. I had both caches down and disposed of in less than thirty minutes."

"Prints?"

Max shook her head. "Too hard to see at night, and with all that slushy mud, there was no way. Even with the full moon, I couldn't see anything worth seeing."

"Hmm." Orren turned in his swivel chair, picking through a file cabinet. "What's up?"

"Wondering if we still had the files on those last poachers. Maybe we could check up on them, do a little stakeout."

"A stakeout? What are you now, a detective?"

"Well if my career here is going down the drain, I'd better get some new skills quick, right?" He pulled a beige file from the drawer and laid it on the desk, flipping through old newspaper articles clipped years back and a faded copy of the police report. "I can look them up, see if they're still in the area."

"Yeah, okay." Max leaned back in her chair, sipping at the terrible coffee. "You really do need to get some sugar in this place. This tastes like sadness and disappointment."

"That's only because you like your coffee pumped full with enough sugar to run an engine for fourteen days straight."

"I don't think engines run on sugar, Orren, in fact I've heard it's pretty important to keep sugar *out* of engines."

"Mhmm." He placed a pair of reading glasses at the end of his nose as he tapped names into the computer's search bar. "Well, none of them have had any other arrests since then."

"Are they still in jail?"

"No, all three released on parole six months ago." He frowned, glancing over at her. "I was hoping you'd be wrong."

"I'm rarely wrong." She sighed. "Not about this. There's no other reason there would be food caches out there two nights in a row."

"There aren't even many wolves left on the mountain."

"Enough to want to protect," Max shot back.

"I never suggested otherwise."

"Well, what now?"

Orren closed the window on the computer and put the file back in the cabinet. "Mr. Parker isn't going to want to hear this right now, not with all the investors on site. You'd be lucky if he didn't send you packing the moment you brought it up."

"Yeah, conservation has never been his top priority. It was a battle getting him to care last time, and that was after three wolves were killed." Max set the empty mug on the desk, planting her palms on her knees. The memory of it hung heavy on her heart, and had ever since it had happened. But it happened outside a full moon, and she was never very good at shifting outside the confines of the lunar cycle. She was powerless, and the wolves had paid the price for her cowardice.

"I can't leave the desk, or he'll know we're up to something," Orren said in a low voice. "All three of them are still local, from what I can tell."

"Still in the next town over?"

Orren nodded. "Looks like it. Probably back working at the tackle shop, if I had to guess."

"It's risky."

"Don't get caught, then." He sucked his teeth, considering his next words. "Take Sloane."

"I'm not taking her."

"You can't go alone, and I'm stuck here so long as there are investors on site. That's going to be the case for a week longer at least, and unless you want these poaches roaming all over the mountain, we need better information. The police won't do anything unless we catch them trespassing."

"What if I just watch the intake road?"

Orren shook his head. "They're foolish, but not so much as to use the same access method twice, especially if they know someone is out there removing the bait traps. I'd guess they might be hiking up one of the old back trails, the ones that have been closed for almost a decade."

"But there are nearly a dozen of those," Max groaned.

"Which is why you need to tail them. Quietly."

"And what good is Sloane going to do, then?"

"Hopefully, keep you from doing something that will get you beat up. You've never been very good at keeping your mouth shut."

"No, it's not a quality I possess."

Orren laughed, standing to add more grounds to the coffee pot. "Plus, they won't recognize her. She's new. You're not. You're the one who got them picked up the last time, I doubt they'll forget your face any time soon."

"I really don't want to admit that you're probably right about this."

"I am most certainly right about this, to the point that if you're not going to take her, if your stubbornness is really that ingrained, I don't think you should go at all."

"Someone has to find out why these creeps are putting bait traps up on the mountain again. I'm not going to stand by and just let it happen all over again." Her fists balled unconsciously at her sides, her short fingernails biting into the soft flesh of her palms. "They can't keep doing this."

"Then Sloane Hearst goes with you."

"What are you going to do, ground me? You can't keep me from going off-site."

"No, but I do have the power to convince Mr. Parker to give you enough extra work that you won't have the time to run off playing petty detective." Orren stood near the door to the back, leaning against the wall with his characteristically relaxed posture. "I know you think I do this to annoy you, but I'm only trying to keep you from getting yourself killed."

"Alright, alright, fine. I'll ask her. What if she says no? We haven't exactly been on the best of terms since she arrived."

"If you could manage to be a little less hostile, I'm betting she won't say no."

Chapter 12

Sloane ran her fingers along the ground, frowning at the lack of snow. She looked up at the cloudless sky with a furrow in her brow, wondering if the whole season was going to be ruined by the high temperatures. The forecast was still suggesting another week of it.

Still sore, still exhausted from the hungry shifts, she hadn't spoken a word to Max the night before. Her bags were neatly stacked in the corner, a surprise, and her sheets had already been changed, which was an almost alarming departure from the hostility she'd been experiencing from the snowboarder from the moment she'd arrived at Crimson Oak.

Her scent dampener was harder to use unnoticed, even though it looked like a normal deodorant. It had a strange smell in the stick before it mixed with her skin chemistry to form a neutrality that would keep her identity as a Bear hidden away. It was unlikely that anyone would know, but her family had always taught her to prioritize caution in the matter.

Yellow grass pushed up through the rocky earth, spiky and crisped against the pads of her fingertips. The investors were still sitting in meetings, and thankfully, Mr. Parker hadn't called for her again. Maybe her lackluster performance the previous day had saved her from any more unwanted, awkward interaction with people who assumed she knew more than she did, all because she had a recognizable name.

"Hey."

Sloane turned, an eyebrow raised. "Carter."

"Inspecting the slopes?"

"Not much else to do. It's a good thing there aren't many guests here, there's no way we can allow anyone out here. Too much danger of erosion if we did."

Max tensed. "I'm aware."

"I'm sorry if I snored last night."

"You didn't."

A strange moment passed, and a crow called from a nearby branch, the brash and brazen song echoing gently down the mountain. "Did you need something?" Sloane asked, a little too tersely.

"Unfortunately."

"Well?"

Max sat down on the ground, pulling at the tufts of dead grass and ripping pieces of it up before tossing them aside. "I want to try tracking the people we think might be trying to poach on the mountain, up near the precipice."

"And how do you think I can help with that? By your own stated facts, you know this place far better than I ever will."

"The people who—who did this last time, about five years ago—they were recently released from prison, and they're still local. I think it might be the same ones."

"Similar methods?"

Max nodded. "Not exactly, but similar enough, yes."

"I still don't know how I fit into this equation."

"Orren said I can't go unless I take you with me. He thinks I'm going to open my big mouth, or get myself punched."

"Oh, so you have a habit of being antagonistic, interesting," Sloane mused aloud, shielding her face from the oppressive sun to stare past the tree line. "And here I thought I was special."

"I'm only antagonistic when it's merited," Max shot back. "It's not easy spending your entire career being looked down on and dismissed by people who think they're better than you, but I'm sure you can't relate."

Sloane gave her a sideways glance. "You'd be surprised."

"I doubt that."

"Male skiers have been at the forefront since forever, ever since we were allowed to start competing. They all think they're better athletes, but really, they're just assholes." Sloane returned her gaze to the woods, squinting past the bright light of midday. "And that's saying nothing about the other women competing. The call is coming from inside the house, you know what I mean?"

"I've never competed professionally, so I wouldn't know."

"You're good enough, I've seen you on the slopes." Sloane swallowed back a yawn, irritated at her own exhaustion. "Or at least, I was seeing you on the slopes, before this damned weather dried everything out."

"I know I'm good enough."

"Then why don't you?"

"Costs money I don't have. You think I can show up to a regional competition in my hand-me-down parka and refurbished board?"

"Oh."

"Yeah, *oh*." Max laughed, and it was derisive. "This is what I mean, princess, these things don't even occur to you. You've led such a charmed, perfect life, one I would have given anything to have, and you don't even act grateful for it."

"I'm aware that I had access to certain privileges thanks to my family." Sloane turned away, her shoulders tightening. "Trust me, they never let me forget it."

"What really happened with the national qualifiers?"

"I don't want to talk about it."

"You'd better start, or the rumor mill will make up their own story."

"I'm aware of that, too."

Max hissed out a sigh, scraping more grass from the loosening dirt. "It doesn't make sense why you'd throw it away for no real reason."

"I had my reasons."

"If I'd gotten that far, there's nothing that would have kept me away. I'd have dragged myself to the piste half dead if I had to, hell, I'd have them strap my coffin to a board if they had to."

"Some things aren't as easy or simple as that."

"Life rarely is, you just have to grab it by the guts and push through. No other way out other than through, not for most of us."

"Mm." Sloane resisted the urge to launch into another tirade, if only because she was too tired to argue. "So when do you want help on this little field trip?"

"It's not a field trip, Hearst, it's an important part of our investigation."

"I didn't realize the local police force had asked us for help."

"They won't do a damned thing unless we catch them in the act. The fact of the matter is, they're probably as corrupt and depraved as the damned poachers are."

"What is there out here to poach?" Sloane asked nonchalantly, already afraid of the answer. "Bears?"

"Wolves mostly, though I'm sure they wouldn't mind a bear. They're trophy hunters, nothing more."

"Are there bears here?"

"Not anymore, and do you want to guess why?"

Sloane flinched. "Poachers?"

"Yeah. There weren't too many to begin with, and now it's been ten years since anyone has seen a black bear in these parts. Maybe down the highway, in the reserve alongside the road, but not on Bear Mountain." Max ripped up another clump of grass. "Ironic, isn't it? No bears on Bear Mountain."

"You shouldn't rip up the grass, it will make the slope uneven when the snow comes in."

"I'm not digging potholes, Hearst, calm down. I swear, you skiers are so uptight, it's a wonder any of you don't crack under the pressure."

"Plenty do."

"I wanted to try to go to the next town over in a couple of days. These guys used to hang out near a fishing tackle shop there."

"In the winter?"

"What, you've never heard of ice fishing?"

Sloane snorted, gesturing around at the mountain. "I don't see much ice, do you?"

"Then I'm sure regular fishing would suffice. Damn, I'm not a fisher, how should I know what they're doing in there? I'm just saying that's where we found them last time, and as far as we can tell, they're still local, so that's the best place to start."

"Okay, so why in a couple of days? Why not go now?"

"I need some time to prepare," Max answered. "Besides, I haven't been sleeping well. I'm tired, and that's a bad combination with a stakeout. We'll need to follow them back here to get evidence it's them. We'll need a camera—"

"I've got one."

"A phone isn't going to be good enough, not at night."

"I have one," Sloane repeated. "I took some lessons last year with this woman who won a wildlife photography competition. She taught me a lot in a weekend, I wound up getting a decent one."

"Expensive hobby to just pick up."

"It was so I could get my own photos for sponsors. Easier than them sending people out all the time, I hate people watching me practice or train."

Max nodded, leaning back on her hands. "Alright. Well, I still need to get some information. I don't completely remember where this place was, not to mention that Orren is all kinds of bent out of shape about this investor visit and potential acquisition."

"Probable acquisition," Sloane corrected. "They seem very motivated."

"Maybe I can motivate them to leave and go find some other place to strip bare and suck the soul out of, what do you think?" Max asked. "Crimson Oak was never meant to be a place for high-level retreats. It should be for everyone."

"Everyone," Sloane repeated.

"Yeah, you don't agree?"

"I never thought about it."

"Have you ever felt like you weren't included? Left behind, closed out of the circle, mocked for it?"

Sloane nodded. "Sure."

"Poor kids deal with that every day, for a million different reasons. Not being able to afford school trips is just one of them. Imagine if this place was lit up with kids from local schools, imagine it creating a new generation of people who love winter sports—but Mr. Parker never went for it, and these new investors sure as hell won't, either."

"Strange that he'd pass up the opportunity for grants to cover the cost."

"I don't think he ever even considered that."

Sloane shrugged. "Probably not. Some lodges are more interested in exclusivity than they are in enriching the next generation."

"What about you?"

"I'm not management material, so I wouldn't know."

"No, I mean—" Max sat upright, straightening her posture. "Do you prefer the exclusive lodges?"

"I prefer nice views and a smooth piste. Beyond that, I couldn't care less."

"I bet the views out west are nicer."

"Nah," Sloane said, looking at her. Max's hair was flopped over onto her face, shiny and dark even in the bright sunlight. Sloane blinked, clearing her throat. Max was frustratingly attractive. Sloane looked away, willing the redness in her cheeks to fade. "It's just as pretty here, just in a different way."

"You should see this place in autumn, it's like the heavens opening up and lighting up all those trees in the distance. Sometimes, when the sun sets, it's almost like fire."

Sloane sat down next to her, looking out over the mountain. "I'd like to see that some day."

"When the investors get their grubby paws on this place, I doubt either of us will be around to see the aftermath."

"Yeah." Sloane grimaced, trying to forget the business card back in their cabin, and the guilt that it wrought deep in her chest. "Maybe that's for the best."

"I wish things were different, I wish—I wish that I could make a change, but I can't. Not really."

"You came out here to ask me to help you track down a pack of poachers, and you think you're not making a difference?"

Max turned away from her, glancing up the slope. "Not enough of one. It sure as hell wasn't enough last time."

"What happened last time?"

"They nabbed a few wolves. We didn't know until it was too late."

"You helped catch them though, right?"

"I guess, but that doesn't change things for the wolves, does it?"

Sloane chewed her lip before answering, biting down hard enough to clear her sleep-fogged thoughts. "No, I guess not."

"It doesn't make any sense, you know?" Max pulled at loose threads around the ripped knees of her cuffed jeans. "I can't even comprehend wanting to do something like that. It feels so pointless."

"I don't know. I've never understood it, either. Bad enough to trophy hunt, much worse when it's a protected species. There aren't many wolves left in the area, are there?"

"Hardly any," Max answered. "Which is why the tragedy of it is so much worse." She took a deep breath, and it was shaky enough to draw Sloane's attention. "There was a mated pair on the mountain then, along with a few cubs." She blew out the rest of the breath before digging her fingers into the ground. "All gone, now."

"Monsters."

"They only got eighteen months. Should have been longer, if you ask me."

"I can't say no to that, can I?" Sloane asked, intentionally avoiding eye contact. "I'm in, but I don't want to get shot at."

"We're just doing recon, Hearst, relax. If we do this right, they won't even know we're there."

"If you say so."

"I'll drive."

"I hope so, otherwise we'd be walking. I don't have a car here, remember?"

"Right, of course. I forgot that you flew in, princess."

"I wouldn't have made it in time if I'd driven across the country." Sloane surveyed the empty slope with a heavy and resigned sigh. "Although, it wouldn't have mattered much, given the state of this place. Not one client for miles."

"What's the count at now, anyway? I think you're one up on me because you stole that first client away for yourself."

"I wish I hadn't."

"Why, because she was a pain in the ass?" Max asked, a touch of anger to her tone.

"In part, but also because I think it set us off on the wrong foot."

"I think you did that when you showed up like you owned the place."

Sloane flashed a glare at her. "Or maybe it was you treating me like some sort of interloper, instead of a colleague."

"Please, I've been around long enough to see how you ski instructors act around people like me. You all want to lord it over me, throwing your weight around, making demands, making snide remarks, acting like you're a gift from the sky above because you can slide down a slope on two slippery sticks."

"And you're better because you can do it on one slippery board?" Sloane asked, incredulous. "All I ever did was show up and try to work, and you've been trying to get in my way from day one. Trying to sabotage me, trying to run me off the property, and for what?" She stood again, brushing the dead grass from her jeans. "For an instructor position that may or may not survive the buyout?"

"First of all, I think you're making a big deal out of nothing. It was just a few towels, it's not like I let a pack of rabid raccoons loose in your cabin."

"*You* did that to my mattress?" Sloane rounded on her, angry breaths shallow in her chest. "I thought that was some guest's kid, not a full-grown adult." She shook her head, heart pounding. "That's the most immature and ridiculous thing I've ever heard."

"What did you mean by trying to run you off, then?"

"Being rude!"

"Please, as if you weren't being just as rude in response." Max averted her eyes, staring into the distance. "And secondly, this might only be an instructor position for you, but this job, this place? It's my entire life. I don't have anything else to fall back on, princess, some of us don't have options like that."

"You could have just said that, then! Instead you decided to prank me like a child. Do you know how long it took me to dry out that mattress? All night I sat there with the hair dryer, trying to air it out enough to sleep on it."

"You could have slept on the floor and aired it out the next day."

"Slept on the floor with what? Those towels soaked through all the sheets, too!"

"You could have used your clothes, then."

"You know what? You're an asshole, Max Carter." Sloane began marching back up the slope, catching her foot and stumbling. "Find the poachers yourself for all I care, I have work to do."

"Wait," Max said, following her up the mountain. "Just wait for a minute, stop angrily marching up the damned mountain!"

Sloane turned on the heel of her boot. "What?" she demanded, raising her shoulders in an exaggerated shrug. "What do you want?"

"I'm—sorry."

"That's it?"

"Maybe soaking the mattress was a little over the line."

"A *little?*"

"It was just some harmless fun," Max replied, shrugging helplessly at her. "Alright, maybe it was to try to get you to leave, but it didn't work, so..." she trailed off, tilting her head to the side. "So I'm sorry. It was immature and I shouldn't have done it."

"Your idea of fun and mine are very different."

"I won't do it again."

"Were you planning to?" Sloane asked, a hand on her hip. When Max didn't reply, she rolled her eyes and turned back towards the summit, climbing purposefully with every enraged step.

"Of course I wasn't planning to, you'd have caught on! I'm honestly surprised I got away with it the first time."

"Got away with it," Sloane hissed, but it wasn't loud enough for Max to hear. At least, she thought it wasn't.

"Listen, I get that you're angry, and I probably would be too, but if you don't come with me, Orren is going to make sure I wind up tied up with a stack of busywork because he's convinced I'll get myself killed."

"With impulses like yours, he's probably right."

"I need you to come with me, or who knows what will happen." Max dragged the toe of her boot along in the dust, kicking up a small cloud. "I don't know if I can have another instance of this weighing on my conscience."

"Fine, I'll come with you. But don't speak to me until we leave. I'm done with you after that, are we clear?" Sloane reached the top of the mountain, and looked down at Max, still making her way back up. "I wouldn't even agree to that much if there weren't innocent animals at risk. Beyond that, I hope I never see you again after this season."

"Fine," Max retorted. "It would be my pleasure."

Chapter 13

Max pulled into a parking space on Main street, a few doors down from the tackle shop. She glanced over at Sloane's stony exterior and cleared her throat quietly. "We're here," she announced, breaking the icy silence. They'd barely spoken five words to each other in two days.

"I gathered as much."

"We have no way of knowing they're in there, unless we go in and look."

"Go look, then."

Max shifted uncomfortably in her seat, turning off the engine with a twist of the key. She sucked her teeth quietly, a noise of contemplation. "They may recognize me from last time."

"Fine, I'll go." Sloane unbuckled herself, throwing open the passenger side door. "Don't leave while I'm in there."

"That would defeat the purpose of this entirely."

"I don't know, it could be another prank, for all I know. Drive out to a town fifteen miles away, and leave me alone to fend for myself. Ha ha, very funny, right?"

Max heaved a sigh. "I already apologized for the mattress."

"And yet, I'm still angry."

"Can you just go inside and look?"

Sloane rolled her eyes, holding a hand out. "Let me see the photos again."

"Here." Max handed over a beige envelope, marked with the Crimson Oak logo stamped on the right hand corner. "Do you remember what Orren told you to say?"

"Yes, I'm looking to upgrade my lake fishing tackle, and need new lures for the spring season." Sloane took the photos out, examining them once again. "Don't you think they'll think it's suspicious I'm preparing for the spring season so early?"

"Not according to Orren."

"I've never been fishing, so I wouldn't know."

"I have, in a sense." Max smirked at her reflection in the rear-view mirror, remembering the time she nabbed the fattest trout she'd ever seen and tore into it as her Wolf form. "It's fun. Invigorating, even, especially if it's more for subsistence than trophies to cast in bronze."

"Three men, two with glasses, one with a tattoo on his left arm, one with a scar across his right eyebrow, one balding." Sloane closed her eyes, nodding her head. "Got it." She opened the door and paused for a moment. "If you're messing with me, and you leave me out here, I will not let you rest for a single moment once I make it back to the mountain."

"I'm not messing with you." Max held up three fingers. "Scout's honor."

"Would a scout drench someone's mattress in winter?"

"Are you ever going to let that go?"

Sloane slammed the door. "No."

"Alright, damn, just go," Max said, sitting back in her seat. She leaned back against the headrest, closing her eyes to the dimming afternoon light. The sunset was going to be an impressive one, purple streaks already encroaching on the pink sky, set against the backdrop of Bear Mountain in the distance, the highest around. Everything else was more or less a hill, with gentle slopes that gradually led down to the lake on the other side of the county.

Main street was quiet, with only the scarce and far-between pedestrian wandering down the cracked sidewalks, deep fissures in the concrete that would take years to be fixed. Max drummed her fingers against the steering wheel, the synthetic leather cool beneath her skin. The forecast was still calling for warmer temperatures, with no signs of snow, and the investors would be making a decision in a week, or so Orren had said.

Maybe the next year at the same time, Max would be back at her retail job, spending eight hours a day getting yelled at by customers too caught up in the frenzied rush to even consider that she might be a person, too. Maybe she'd have given up and laid in a ditch somewhere, letting the rainwater and mud reclaim her, because some days sacrificing herself to become fertilizer seemed like a better option than the job she had back home, one that drained her, moment by moment, as though every second she spent in that store was taking years off her life.

Sloane was gone for less than ten minutes when she returned to the car, reusable tote bag in hand, filled with fishing tackle. "It's them."

"You weren't supposed to actually buy the tackle, Hearst."

"It looked less suspicious that way. Besides, maybe this will inspire me to take up a new hobby."

"You like seafood?"

"Yeah." She buckled her seatbelt, nodding at the road. "Let's go."

"Go where? We're supposed to be tailing them."

"Yeah, and if you'd open those enormous hazel eyes of yours, you'd see that all three of them are about to leave the establishment."

"Do you think you tipped them off?" Max asked.

"They barely noticed me, I doubt it. Look, there they are, getting into that truck."

"Nice truck."

Sloane snorted. "Yeah, and not a speck of dirt on it. I bet that thing has never seen a day of work in its life."

"It looks almost brand new."

"Are you going to follow them, or what?"

"Yes," Max said, irritation creeping in at the edges of her tone. "But I'm going to at least try not to be so obvious as to sit right behind them the whole way there, wherever they are going."

"Don't lose them."

"I'm not going to lose them!"

"Look, they're turning left at that stop sign."

Max followed suit, rolling through the intersection with nothing more than a slight pause. "Yes, I have eyes, I can see them."

"If you keep doing that, you're going to get pulled over."

"If I'd have known you'd be such a backseat driver, I would have left you at

Crimson Oak barred in the cabin and lied to Orren about it."

"Please, as if that would have worked. I could have just screamed until someone let me out, and then where would you be?"

"At least I wouldn't be in this car with you," Max grumbled under her breath.

"What was that?"

"Nothing."

Sloane leaned forward in her seat, getting as close to the windshield as she could, watching the shining silver truck as it turned onto another side street. "Where could they be going? They're not headed towards the mountain."

"If I had to guess, they're going to the local bar. It's about seven blocks up on the right."

"Drinking and bear baiting, what a combination."

Max glanced at her. "Wolf baiting," she corrected.

"Right, of course. Sorry, I misspoke."

"See, they're pulling over. Looks like we're in for a long night, although, I don't know why I expected anything different. Nothing else to do in this town other than drink." Max drove past the truck, edging her car slowly over the speed bump in the road, waiting until they entered the bar to park another block up. "Stay here."

"What are you doing? Orren said they'd recognize you!"

"I want to make sure it's them."

"It is them, I told you."

"Just let me check it out. For all we know, they know we're onto them and might already be climbing out a back window."

"If they don't already know we're onto them, they sure as hell will as soon as you waltz in there with your recognizable face!"

Max sighed, unbuckling herself. "Just stay here, I'll only be gone a few minutes."

"What was even the point of me coming out here with you, if you're just going to do whatever you want anyway?"

"I know this town better than you, and I know these people better than you."

"Why, because you spend a few months out of the year up at the mountain?" Sloane asked, moving to unbuckle her own seat belt. "That's hardly a rousing endorsement."

"It's more than you." Max opened the door and sighed. "I won't go inside, I just want to look from the street side window. If they're just sitting at the bar, then I'll come back, and we can wait in painfully awkward silence until they leave to head up the mountain."

"Fine."

"Fine," Max agreed, shoving her hands into her pockets after slamming the door shut. The little side street was almost abandoned, with plenty of shuttered stores and nothing more than dusty for rent signs in their front windows. With the new Syndicorp superstore that opened just a mile up the road, most people had no reason to spend time in the town anymore, and people had already begun to move away. One more ghost town, more empty buildings, more people who'd been left behind by *progress*, if it could even be called that.

The bar was one of those old local haunts, where the neon sign outside was half busted, only the letters b and a lit, the r remaining dark. The wood cladding above the door was covered in layers of cracked, peeling blue paint, and there was a sticker on the window from the college team's football win from ten years prior. The town had been different then, more vibrant, but times had changed, and along with them, the quiet encroachment of the inevitable.

She crept alongside the window, crouching near to the sidewalk, peering inside. She squinted against the gentle tint of the glass into the dark bar, and spotted all three of them drinking beer at the counter, half watching the basketball game on the small television that hung in the corner. Max sighed, turning away. They were just drinking, the same as Sloane had said they would be. Max had almost expected them to be looking back at her, as though they'd been waiting for her all along.

The light was fading fast now, and the absence of the artificial glow of street lamps was palpable. They stood, tall and iron and unused, their bulbs long since darkened by budget cuts. With no one on the street, there was no need to waste local funds to power them. No light meant even those who tried to come back to the town were pushed away, especially during the short days of winter.

Max approached her car, ready to climb in, but stopped short when she saw Sloane with a phone to her ear and a hand pressed to her forehead. Max hesitated, unsure if she should just get back into the car anyway, or wait in an alley. She waited so long to make the decision that she found herself just standing there, listening and wishing she wasn't.

"No, Mom, I told you, I'll figure it out when I get back," Sloane said, her voice gently muffled by the rolled up windows. "I can't help how qualifiers turned out, you know that. What was I supposed to do? It's not like I could have just pushed through—no, I couldn't have pushed through, it would have risked everything—Mom, I've tried telling you before, I *did* ask them to move the dates back to their original set."

Max shifted in place, feeling like she should leave, but somehow, still stood rooted to the spot.

"I'm sorry, okay? I did my best and it wasn't good enough, and that was that." Sloane laid a clenched fist on the dashboard, holding the phone away from her ear. "No, I don't get service up on the mountain, I told you that." She laid her head back on the rest now, eyes closed, and Max was sure she'd open them and see her. Sloane sighed heavily. "I know this isn't how you saw things going for me, but—"

The sound of the bar's door opening spurred Max into action, and she dove into the nearby alley. Two women she'd never seen before passed on the street, stumbling and giggling, before climbing into a waiting car. Max turned back to her own car, alarmed to see Sloane brushing tears from her eyes.

"I don't know what else to say. Listen, we're heading back up the mountain now, I'm going to lose you anyway. I'll call when I can." Sloane laid the phone face down in her lap and leaned her forehead against the dashboard, resting on her forearm.

Max coughed loudly as she approached the car, dragging her boots across the concrete sidewalk to announce her presence and give Sloane enough time to gather herself.

"So," Max said, sliding back into her seat and closing the door. "It's them."

"I told you it was."

"We'll just have to wait for them to be done, but it might be a while. There's a game on, and it only started about ten minutes ago."

"It's not like I have anywhere else to be," Sloane replied flatly.

"I know the feeling."

"I should be preparing for nationals right now, not waiting to follow some drunk assholes down the road." Sloane turned, and her normally porcelain face was red and blotchy. "Snowboarders ruin everything."

"I'm sorry?"

"Their inclusion in nationals this year is why my qualifier date got pushed. I got... sick. If the dates had stayed the same as they were when they were announced, I'd be training in Aspen."

"I wasn't aware that individual snowboarders had any say over qualifier timetables," Max shot back, her sympathy fading fast. "You've got a hell of a chip on your shoulder, and you need to get over it."

"I do? What about *you?* You think you know everything there is to know about me, and you've thought that from the moment you laid eyes on me."

"I could say the same thing to you."

Sloane sighed angrily, laying her palms flat against her knees. "This isn't how my life was supposed to go."

"Welcome to the club, princess."

"I was supposed to be somebody."

"Weren't we all?" Max asked. "Weren't we all sold the same story? Weren't we all pushed down paths we didn't belong on?"

"I did belong on that path. I was about to make the national team. I was going to make a name for myself."

"And then what?"

"What do you mean, *and then what?*" Sloane hissed.

"You and I both know that's not a career forever. You get five, maybe seven good years if you start early enough, and then what? Your knees give out, you take a bad spill, and they all toss you to the side like garbage. Best you can hope for is hosting the meets a few times a year, but beyond that?" Max took a pack of mints from the pocket of her hoodie, popping one into her mouth. "Beyond that, there's a lot of has-beens with nothing other than stories about the glory days."

Sloane stared at her. "What else is there, if not that?"

"I don't know. If I figure it out, I'll let you know." Max offered her the tin, and she took one. "There has to be more than this, but so far, it's all I've got."

"They've barely spoken to me since I pulled out of the qualifiers."

"Who?"

"My family." Sloane moved the mint around in her mouth slowly, considering her words. "My parents think I should have done the qualifiers anyway."

"Why didn't you?"

"I was sick. I wouldn't have performed well, it would have been more embarrassing than pulling out."

"Sick with what?" Max asked.

"Does it matter?"

"I don't know, I guess not."

Sloane bit into the mint with a soft crunch. "It was a stomach bug."

"Hard to be on the slopes like that."

"Impossible. Can you even imagine?"

"Bad timing." Max glanced at her before checking her rear view mirror. "But blaming snowboarders isn't going to help."

"It feels like it will. Easier to have someone to blame that isn't myself. It makes looking in the mirror slightly less painful."

"My family never really got it, either. We don't talk much."

"They didn't want you to go pro?"

"They didn't want me to leave town, more like. It was good enough for them, so why wasn't it good enough for me?"

Sloane rubbed her hands against her knees, brushing quietly against the dark denim. "I was supposed to be someone different. Someone who went pro, lined up sponsorships, did those panel commentator gigs you mentioned, got married, settled down, had kids. I don't know, it feels like now that I've failed the first hurdle, everything else is drifting away."

"Did you ever really want any of that stuff, or did your family want it for you?"

"It's hard to tell."

"Is that the real reason you're all the way out here in the Midwest at Crimson Oak? Running from your problems?"

"It was too late in the season to get in anywhere else, the shorter season here gave me an opening." Sloane picked at the zipper on her jacket. "But yes, the distance has been nicer than I might have imagined."

"It's too bad only one of us gets to stay the whole season."

"Mr. Parker is a fool."

"He is, but he's the fool with the property deed, so what can you do?" Max asked, resigned to her own fate now. "He should be running longer seasons when the weather isn't like this, community events, applying for grants, other activities, the works. But he's let it grow stagnant, just like all the towns around here."

"I'm not sure he has many options, not without investment capital."

"He's tired and wants an easy out, and I can't blame him, especially not this year when it looks like a summer meadow up on the piste."

Sloane bounced her knee nervously, checking the side mirrors before she spoke again. "How long do we wait for these clowns?"

"As long as it takes."

"I can't believe someone would go up on Bear Mountain just to poach."

"Believe it, because it already happened once, and obviously, they're trying again." Max sighed, running her hands over the steering wheel. "At least, I hope it's them, otherwise we don't have any real leads as to who's up there causing problems."

"Then let's hope they're done soon, because I'm getting bored staring at the side mirrors."

"You'd never make it as a detective, Hearst," Max said with a light chuckle. "One hour into a stakeout, and you're ready to throw in the towel."

"The drenched, half-frozen towel."

"Alright, alright. I hear you."

Sloane gave her a sideways glance. "Someone should do that to you someday, see how you like it."

"Someone has."

"Oh yeah? Who? A little sister, maybe?"

Max winced. "No. I haven't seen my little sister in ten years." She poked the radio's power button, desperate to fill the silence with something other than the tension that had settled between them once again. "It was a ski instructor, my first year teaching at Crimson Oak."

"Oh."

"And then again the second, third, and fourth years, until I gave them all a run for their money."

"What did you do?"

"I worked twice as hard as any of them. I built out my roster of clients, I showed up early and left late." Max smirked. "And I might have frozen all the locks on their cars."

"Harsh."

"Nah. Ten minutes with a hair dryer and they were right as rain. It taught them to stop messing with me, though."

Sloane shifted in her seat, the soft friction of jacket against upholstery an underpinning note to the irritatingly jangly rendition of a festive carol being pushed through the car's speakers. "Why did you mess with me, then?"

"Preemptive action."

"I hadn't done anything to you."

"Other than accusing me of carving up the slopes, and looking down your cute little nose at me, the same way all the others had." Max sighed, leaning her head back and examining the small scuffs on the ceiling of the car. "Do we really have to keep going over this?"

"No."

"Good."

A quiet moment came and went, along with the carol on the radio, and Max twisted the knob, looking for another station. That far up in the hills, there weren't any others, and she resigned herself to it, twisting back to the station they'd left. A cover of a slow ballad was starting, and she huffed quietly, cursing herself for not buying a new adapter for her phone.

"I wasn't looking down my nose at you," Sloane said.

"I've been around long enough to recognize disdain when it's staring me in the face," Max replied, frowning at the radio's betrayal.

"I was fresh off of pulling out of nationals qualifiers, excuse me for not being princess-like and cordial."

"Oh, you're a princess alright, just not cordial."

"Let's just watch the door."

"Fine with me."

Chapter 14

Sloane drummed her fingers against the dash of the car, impatient after an hour and a half of stony silence. Every time she thought she was getting through to her, she walled up again, and so she let the overly enthusiastic festive music fill the gap, trying not to resent it for what it was, another reminder that she wouldn't really be welcome home until she made something of herself. That much had been made perfectly clear.

For the three-hundredth time that minute, she checked the side mirrors, but this time, instead of an empty street, she saw the bar's door open, and the three poachers stumbled out of the car.

"Hey," Sloane hissed, elbowing Max in the side.

"Ouch! What?"

"Look, they're leaving."

Max twisted in her seat, squinting into the growing darkness. Night fell fast in December, this far north. "Shit." She started the car, turning the headlights on, and then off.

"What are you doing?"

"They might notice us if we keep the headlights on."

"We might die if you keep them off, have you lost your senses?" Sloane demanded, buckling her seatbelt.

Max responded with an exasperated sigh. "Just until they pull off the street, relax, alright? Like Orren said, these three probably haven't forgotten my face. I don't want to give them any cause to remember it, alright?"

"Yeah, alright, fine." Sloane gripped the handle on her side of the car, bracing her body, pushing herself as far back into the seat as she could go.

"You look like you're preparing for a rocket launch, Hearst, and not a twenty mile an hour drive through the abandoned streets of a ghost town."

"Plenty of damage can be done at that speed."

"We're not on skis, we're in a car that was built twenty years ago and has survived this far, I think we're fine. I don't intend on aiming for anything solid." Max released the parking brake. "Besides, I have very good night vision."

"Not as good as mine, I'm betting," Sloane mumbled in reply.

"What was that?"

"Nothing."

Max eased the car into gear, watching the three men as they stumbled across the road. "You should be more worried about them than me," she said acerbically. "Not one of them looks sober enough to drive."

"Why do you think I'm so concerned about tailing them? Not only are they going to drive like fools, if they catch us, there's no telling what they'll do."

"Look, they're getting into that truck."

Sloane peered out the window, watching as each of them climbed into the truck, the driver pausing to retch into a barren bush. "Charming," she said, her own stomach roiling at the sight of it.

"Princes, all of them. It's a wonder they haven't all been snapped up by the landed gentry of the area to be given a life of leisure." Max snorted. "Maybe one of them could be your dream come true, Princess."

"I've always been one for the other princesses, actually."

Max raised an eyebrow. "Aren't you full of surprises?"

"Please, it's not as though it's not *painfully* obvious." Sloane met her glance and tilted her head. "What's the matter, Carter, your gaydar need adjusting?"

"Apparently."

"Are you going to follow them, or what?" Sloane asked, looking back over her shoulder at the truck as it pulled away from the curb. "They're turning left down that street."

"Yes, okay, of course I'm going to follow them, just give me a second!" Max replied, turning the car around in the dead end of the road. "I don't want to look quite so obvious as to be tailgating them, alright?"

"They're going to get away if you don't hurry up!"

"Great, next time you can be the driver when we're stalking dangerous poachers."

"Gladly! At least then we'd know where they are!"

Max pulled the car around the corner, nodding towards the intersection three streets ahead, the red of their brake lights glowing in the surrounding night. "See, they're right there, I didn't lose them." She frowned as the truck ahead swerved from side to side. "Yikes," she said quietly.

"Should we call the police?"

"They're at least twenty minutes away, there's no way they'd get out here in time. Let's see where they're going, if it's the mountain, we'll have our proof."

"Right turn," Sloane announced.

"Yes, I can see, thank you."

"I'm just trying to be helpful."

"Be quiet, that's helpful." Max followed the truck down another road, easing her car behind them from a safe distance. "This isn't the way to the mountain."

"Didn't you say there were back roads? Lots of them?"

"Not out this way, it's the wrong direction. There are only houses up this way."

Sloane's eyes followed the truck, matching Max's stare of consternation. "Are they—" she squinted, leaning forward towards the dashboard. "Are they parking?"

"Looks like it." Max cut the engine, hands still poised on the keys in the ignition. "Maybe they stalled it?"

"Or they live out this way."

"Damn."

Sloane stared through the glass, and the three men exited the truck, all stumbling into one of the houses, past the wrought-iron fence and the immaculately tended front garden, the miniature conifers perfectly symmetrical. "They're done for the night, I think."

"Yeah."

"If they are the poachers, then at least there won't be any poaching tonight?"

"And if they aren't, then we just left the mountain basically unguarded for hours," Max said, starting the car again. "Come on, we should get back. Orren will want to know we didn't get ourselves killed."

"Do you think there could be other poachers in the area?" Sloane asked. She'd been out on that mountain in full Polar Bear form, and to think she'd been that close to danger made bile rise up in the back of her throat.

"Maybe. The methods were different this time, but I thought maybe they'd just decided to try something different, throw people off the scent." Max pulled the car onto the small highway that led back to the mountain. "Though, given how they hid those caches, or rather, didn't hide them, I don't think they anticipated anyone would be out there looking."

"Caches?" Sloane asked.

"Food caches."

"In the woods?"

Max gave her an exasperated look. "Yeah, Hearst, in the woods. Where the hell else would they be trying to bait wolves, in the lodge's parking lot, in full view of the cameras?"

"Right." Sloane had to bite back a laugh, realizing what had happened. Max must have been hiking that second night, and found the caches she'd left. One night lost to a wolf, another lost to a human. So much for spending a couple of full moons relatively undisturbed. "Maybe it wasn't poachers?"

"Why else would someone be leaving that much salmon in the woods?"

It was a fair question, and not one Sloane could give a believable answer to without giving away what she really was. "To feed the wolves? Out of the kindness of their hearts?"

"That may be the most naive thing I have ever heard."

"So what, then? Different poachers? Is Bear Mountain *the* spot for poaching?"

"It's not impossible they got a tip from somewhere, maybe even those fools we were tracking back there." Max smacked her hand against the steering wheel. "I should have known it wasn't them. Last time it was fish heads and entrails, you know, cheap, free stuff they could get from a fishmonger or a butcher. This time it was planks of fresh salmon, looked fresh that day."

"Seems like a waste if you're just trying to poach, no?"

"Not if you're trying to make sure a wolf shows up." Max shook her head, turning on the high beams as the street lights went dark along the side of the road. "Hardly any wolves left around these parts, I don't even know if there are any on the mountain anymore. Not after what happened last time."

"There are, I saw one," Sloane blurted out, internally cursing herself and her big mouth.

"What? When?"

"Oh, you know," she trailed off, waving a hand casually in the air. "I went for a night hike a few evenings ago."

"When?"

"I don't know, earlier in the week."

"What night?"

"Does it matter?" Sloane asked, and clamped her jaw shut at the sharp tone in her own voice.

"Yes, actually, it does, because you might have been out there when the poachers were out there. What kind of wolf? What time were you out there, did you see anything?"

"Don't you think I would have said something already if I'd seen something out there?"

"Well, I don't know, you certainly waited this long to tell me that you saw a wolf in the woods."

Sloane shrugged. "I didn't think that would be a big deal. It's not unheard of for wolves to be in these parts."

"But after I mentioned poachers?"

"I assumed you knew there was a wolf out there, otherwise why would you be so angry about poachers? If there weren't any wolves in the woods, what else would they be poaching?"

"I—I don't know," Max said, the steering wheel fiercely gripped in her hands. "It's the principle of the thing. If they're out there baiting with food caches, who's to say wolves don't show up? Or bears, for that matter?"

"I definitely didn't see any bears on the mountain," Sloane said carefully. Not technically a lie, as she hadn't been very interested in seeking out her own reflection.

"I think the food caches might have been drugged."

"What?"

"It would make sense for poachers to do that, to sedate whatever they were hunting. Makes it easier to get a clean shot, you know."

"How do you know it was drugged?"

Max sucked her teeth, eyes firmly fixed on the road. "I just have a feeling."

She was so wrong that it hurt, but Sloane kept her mouth shut anyway. "Okay, and what did you do with the caches when you found them?"

"I threw them away."

All that salmon, wasted. Sloane's stomach growled in protest, still perpetually famished from two nights of hungry shifting. "Right. That makes sense."

"What did you think I would do with it, leave it there?"

"No, I was just wondering. I haven't had many run-ins with poachers." That much was true—the lodges she tended to frequent had much better security, more seclusion, and nearly always had an area off limits to guests at all times that worked well for a quiet, unobtrusive shift.

"Lucky you."

"My great-aunt did, though. She barely escaped a pack of poachers with her life." Sloane punctuated her statement with a quiet sigh. Aunt Nell had never been the same after that, at least, that's what everyone else in the family said.

"Where was that?"

"Alaska, I think."

"Colder than here, I'll bet." Max was still hunched over the steering wheel, still tense and keyed up, the stress of it clearly visible in her every movement. "As if the weather wasn't enough of a problem to deal with this season, we've got mystery poachers now, too."

"What about asking Mr. Parker for extra security?"

"Please, he's too busy padding the bottom line, hoping to snare those investors into paying more for Crimson Oak than what it's really worth."

"Trail cameras?" As soon as the words left Sloane's mouth, she regretted it. She'd have at least one more full moon at Crimson Oak, maybe more if she stayed on, and cameras would definitely pick up a huge, hulking polar bear that was thousands of miles away from where it should be.

"No," Max replied firmly, much to Sloane's surprise. "Poachers will only take them down."

"Right, of course," Sloane replied, relieved that her impulsive comment hadn't been taken seriously. "I think I've heard of that happening."

"Often."

"What are we going to do when we get back?"

"Talk to Orren, and then I don't know, maybe I'll take a hike, see if anyone has laid out any more food caches."

"I can help."

"Are you volunteering?"

Sloane shrugged, despite the fact that Max wasn't looking at her. "It's not like I have anything else better to do."

"You don't know the trails."

"I know them well enough. What do you think I spend my time doing when there are no clients—which, lately—is all of the time?"

"Making paper snowflakes to hang in the main hall would have been my guess."

"That only took a few hours."

"It wouldn't surprise me if you're still adding to it, trying to woo Mr. Parker into keeping you on instead of me."

"I never told him it was me that finished the decorations. He never asked."

"Get used to that, because that is how the man operates. So long as things get done, he doesn't care who did it or why. But if something doesn't get done, then brace yourself for a long speech about how long Crimson Oak has been in his family, how we should have pride of tradition when we work there and our main goal should be to uphold the tenets of blah, blah, blah."

"If it would just snow, we could both have enough clients to keep us more than busy, and at least it would pass the time until this buyout is done."

Max's jaw set firm, flexing against her cheeks. "Yeah," she finally said, pulling onto the lodge's narrow road. "Until the buyout is done."

"I didn't mean it like that, only that—"

"Yes, you did. You see me leaving as an inevitability."

Sloane scoffed, looking out the window over moon-drenched fields in the valley. "No I don't, I never said that."

"Please, you've known from the moment that was announced that you'd leave here the victor."

"I don't want to argue about this again."

"Why, because I'm right?"

"No, because I'm tired of rehashing the same points over and over again. What good does that do? Neither of us can change his mind, at least, as far as I can tell."

Max cracked a knuckle as the car slowly scaled the slope of the road. "I would give everything to not have to leave this place. It's the only place that has ever felt like home to me."

Gravel crunched softly beneath the tires, and Sloane stayed silent, trying her best to swallow back the guilt that was burning high in her chest, as though she'd eaten something too spicy, but it was her own conscience fanning the flames.

"I guess I can't expect you to understand, you've spent time at dozens of different lodges, I'm betting."

"None like this one."

"Why is that, fewer cocktails rimmed with actual gold?"

"I guess in part it's the facilities, but it's also the quiet, the peace of mind, the lack of... expectations."

"I'd love to have expectations like yours. Show up for fancy galas, for photo shoots, the daunting responsibility of being a well-known skier who's had everything handed to her on a silver platter."

"The expectation to get into nationals or be ignored."

Max glanced at her. "Who's ignoring you?"

"It doesn't matter."

It was Max's turn to fall silent, and the car crested the hill, coming to a stop in the parking lot in front of the main hall. The moon, not quite full anymore, was half covered by delicate, wispy clouds, the kind without snow in them, the kind that looked beautiful in photographs and paintings, but wouldn't solve Crimson Oak's seasonal problems.

"I'll go talk to Orren," Sloane announced, desperate to get out of the car. That had been plenty of sharing for one day, especially with a woman she was pretty sure still despised her. She unbuckled herself, slamming the door behind her. Sloane crossed in front of the main hall, the twinkling lights sparkling from the inside, and she cautiously opened the door to reception. "Orren?" she called, opening it wider. "Orren, we're back."

He lifted his head off the desk, wiping away a delicate string of drool. "What happened?" he asked, sitting up. "Where's Max?"

"She's in the parking lot. We found them, but all they did was get drunk and drive to someone's house. If there are poachers on the mountain tonight, it's not them." She chewed her lip, unsure of how far she should help the lie along. "We're going to hike the woods to see if there are any other signs out there."

"Now? It's not far off eleven at night!"

"You were happy to let us stalk poachers, but walking in the forest at night is where you draw the line?"

He glared at her first, and then laughed. "You're as bad as Max is."

"What?"

"I won't even bother trying to stop you, you have a look in your eye that tells me you're going to go out there regardless of what I say." He pulled a walkie-talkie from the desk drawer and tossed it to her. "Here, at least take this. Call if something happens."

"I will definitely call you if we wind up dead."

"If you both wind up dead, I'll have a lot of paperwork to do, so I'd prefer if the call came prior to reanimation."

"Oh, Orren, zombies aren't real. Don't be ridiculous."

"That's what they said about Werewolves, too, but here I sit."

Sloane stared at him, blinking. "You what?" she stammered, bracing herself on the back of the chair to steady her unsure legs.

"You look like you just saw a ghost, Sloane. It was a joke."

"A joke. Right."

"Did you really think I was being serious? A Werewolf? Come on, be realistic."

"No, of course not," she said brightly, waving him away with a smile. "I was messing with you."

"If you're not back by midnight, I'm going to assume you're dead." He nodded at the small radio with an arched eyebrow. "Don't wind up dead. We'd have reporters here, and Mr. Parker will be upset that his big deal got steamrolled."

"Noted." Sloane clipped the radio to her belt loop, one hand on the door knob. "You should get back to your cabin. We'll radio when we're back at ours."

"Don't kill each other, either. Even more paperwork for me then."

"I'll do my best." She waved, closing the door behind her. Max was already marching towards the woods, no hesitation at all in her gait. "Hey Carter, where do you think you're going?" she called across the yellow-green of the grass.

"You were taking too long."

"You might be the most impatient person I've ever met." Sloane jogged to catch up with her, matching her pace when she did. "Orren gave us a walkie in case we find anything."

"What is he going to do about it, file another report that never gets followed up on?" Max asked, ducking beneath a low-hanging pine bough. "Pointless."

"I think it's more if we come across *people*, Max." There was a crispness in the air that hadn't been there before, and Sloane breathed it in deep. "What is Max short for, anyway?"

"Maxine."

"You don't seem like a Maxine."

"No? You sure as hell seem like a Sloane."

"What's that supposed to mean?"

Max tilted her head, examining a print in the mud. "It means people like your parents tend to like names like yours."

"You've never even met my parents."

"I can make some guesses that I'm betting are right on the money."

"Okay, then prove it."

"You went to private school. Boarding school, maybe," Max said, and gave her a questioning look.

Sloane nodded. "I did."

"Are all the stories true?"

"Yes."

Max laughed, and it echoed gently over the old bark of the trees, the sound quickly deadened by the damp leaves underfoot. "I bet they have fancy dishes for dinner parties."

"Admittedly, yes."

"And they have offshore accounts paired with a creative accountant."

Sloane followed close behind her. "I don't know the specifics."

"Also a yes, then." Max paused again, rubbing a leaf between two fingers. "I also bet they hate each other."

"Not publicly."

"No, never that, imagine what people would say," Max said in a mocking tone, but sobered when she saw the look on Sloane's face. "Sorry."

"It's fine."

"Siblings?"

"No."

"An only child too," Max said, glancing up at the sky. "Sometimes I wish I'd been one, too."

Sloane let the moment pass as they wound up in a small, natural clearing. "Orion's belt," she announced, catching that Max was also staring up at the stars. "And a nice view of Ursa Major."

"They never could tell me for sure whether the mountain was named for actual bears, or for the view up here of that constellation."

"Maybe both." Sloane sat on the cold ground, feeling moisture wick into the denim of her jeans, deciding to ignore the discomfort of it. "You can just about see it, almost, if you squint."

"See what?"

"The Great Orion Nebula. A little blurry with the naked eye. Imagine getting a good telescope up here, it would be amazing."

"What are you, some kind of closeted astronomer?"

"I've spent a lot of time looking up at the sky," Sloane answered as Max sat down next to her. "Sirius," she said, pointing in a line east from the belt. "Canis Major. And Aldeberan, a red supergiant."

"What else?" Max asked, following her motions.

"Pleiades, but better with binoculars at least."

"I'm fresh out of binoculars."

"Capella is up there, over Orion's head. South, Procyon in Canis Minor."

"Do you like dogs?" Max asked.

"Uh, sure? I haven't ever really thought about it. I've always been on the road too much to settle down like that." Sloane leaned back on her hands, her fingers digging into soft loam. "But yeah, I've met some good ones."

"I always imagined what it would be like to live on this mountain, holing up in some little cabin, a dog wandering alongside me through the woods." Max sat down next to her, legs stretched out.

"Sounds idyllic."

"It's a pipe dream."

"Sometimes dreams come true," Sloane said, tossing a rock into a nearby bush. "Just not for me."

"What's your dream, then?" Max asked. "What is the thing that grabs you by the lungs and makes you feel like you'll die without it?" She glanced over at Sloane, and in that waning moon's light, she looked otherworldly. Magical, almost, in a fae-like way. "What does Sloane Hearst think about, when no one else is watching?"

"I used to know." Sloane turned away, trying to blink back the tears that pricked at the corners of her eyes. "I don't think I do anymore."

"There will be another try for nationals in four years."

"Nah. I'll be old news by then."

"It's not unheard of, common even, these days." Max picked up a stick, snapping it into tiny pieces. "I haven't given up on going pro yet, neither should you."

"I don't know if I want to go pro." Sloane said it so quietly, she was almost surprised when Max turned to face her, staring her down.

"Really?"

"Yeah."

"Since when?"

Sloane swallowed hard, willing away the hard lump in her throat. "Since always, maybe."

"Why did you do it for so long, then?"

"It was expected of me. I didn't know what else I could do, if I was even good at anything else. It was easier to go with the flow of others' expectations, I guess."

"That sounds pretty miserable."

"I guess it was. Is."

Max looked up at the sky again, her eyes darting from star to star. "If you don't want to go pro, then you should quit."

"It's not that easy."

"Isn't it?"

"No!" Sloane pressed the heels of her hands into her eyes, trying to stem the unbidden flow that threatened to cascade down her cheeks, a betrayal of her elusive calm. "No," she repeated, "it's not that easy. People will want to know why, and they'll want answers, and people will talk, and make judgments, and gossip, and spread rumors about why I left the sport."

"Do you even like skiing?"

"Yes."

"What do you like about it?"

Sloane sighed heavily, and it caught in her throat. "The freedom."

"Yeah." Max nodded. "I get that."

"There's significantly less freedom, though, when you're trying to make nationals."

"I think competition brings out my best edge. I'm never more alive than I am when I'm absolutely tearing up the slopes, when I'm beating the pants off someone who thought they were better than me."

"You're motivated by spite."

Max snorted. "I guess you could say that. It's not like I could be motivated by much else. My family..." she trailed off and huffed out a sigh. "The less said about them, the better."

"I sometimes wish that I hadn't showed any talent in skiing, that it could have stayed a hobby. Maybe I'd be doing something else, somewhere else, and it would be something I did a few times a year just for the fun of it, dusting off my skis for a weekend trip away."

Max leaned over, bumping their shoulders together. "What, are you saying you'd rather be anywhere other than here with me?"

"Oh." Sloane turned, and was surprised to see Max looking at her like that. No one had ever looked at her quite like that before, and she almost gave into the urge to jerk away. She took a deep breath and as she exhaled, pressed their shoulders closer together. "No," she answered quietly. "I wouldn't say that."

"What are you saying, then?"

"That I wish I was someone different."

"I don't know, you're not so bad, once you get past the princessy attitude." Max arched an eyebrow and smirked. "But, you know, some people are into that."

"Some people."

"What's the matter, Hearst, don't you have a whole horde of princessy friends back in Aspen?"

Sloane chewed on the inside of her cheek. "When we were down the mountain tonight, I checked my phone again. I checked yesterday when I was in town with Bev, and I checked tonight, and not a single one of them has texted me about pulling out of nationals." She dug the heels of her boots down into the soft, muddy earth. "None of them have texted me at all. Not a voice message, not even a sad face emoji."

"Then they weren't really your friends."

"I guess not."

"People like that are what I have a problem with. The ones who stick around just to see how much they can squeeze out of you before they disappear." Max tilted her head. "It's bullshit, Sloane."

"Yeah."

"I don't have many friends back home, either. Orren is the closest thing I have to a real friend, and he only tolerates me because he's paid to."

"Nah, he likes you."

"He's a fool," Max replied, laughing, and she threw her head back and laughed some more, and Sloane couldn't pull her eyes away. When Max stopped, their glances met, and neither looked away. "*I'm* a fool," Max whispered.

Max leaned forward and kissed her before either of them could rethink it. Their lips met, soft and warm on a night that was supposed to be colder but wasn't, under a moon that had the power to tear all of it apart if Sloane made one wrong move. All it would take was one misstep, one tiny error, and everything in her life would turn into a specular, devastating explosion.

Sloane pulled away, shaking her head. "I'm sorry," she said, standing up. She dropped the radio on the ground, turning, leaving a deep gash in the mud. She left Max sitting in the clearing, alone, the guilt of it already curling around her chest like razor wire.

Chapter 15

It had been a week, three days, and approximately two and a half hours since Max had kissed Sloane, and they'd barely spoken a word to each other. They passed each other in practical silence every morning, moving around the other like a ghost or a polite poltergeist, occasionally knocking something over out of clumsiness but always replacing it where it had been, always casting a sideways glance to see if the other was looking, always being left a little emptier when she wasn't.

She shouldn't have kissed her, but she had, and she was paying the price for it. The cost was ten days of terse exchanges, and with every day that passed without a single meaningful syllable uttered, Max became more and more convinced they'd never see each other again after the season was over.

The woods at night were peaceful, or at least, they had been, once. Max trudged through the mud, the beam of the flashlight trained on the ground for every step to keep her from tripping over tree roots or unseen obstacles. She'd been walking a different route every night, looking for more signs of the poachers and finding none. Not a single food cache, or footprint, or tire track, or old, burned out campfire. Just as quickly as they'd appeared, they were gone again, and the unpredictability of it roiled the bile in her stomach.

Were they trying to keep her off-guard? Or maybe it had been the same poachers, but they'd seen them that night in town, scaring them off with the unsaid threat of a parole officer getting tipped off. Or maybe she'd hallucinated the entire thing—after all, she'd seen a polar bear that night, and those certainly weren't hanging around in the Midwest. Not outside of the cages in zoos, anyway.

She let loose a quiet grunt of frustration, again finding nothing in the woods. If there had been food, she'd have found it, combing over every inch of the forest in the dark, poised and waiting for a threat that never came. Max shifted her stance in the mud, her boots already caked in it. Still no snow, and the weather not showing any signs of improvement, but the town at the bottom of the mountain was still alight with the delicate, multi-colored blink of lights, barely visible beyond a vague halo from that altitude.

Clients had been far and few between, and she was spending most of her days in the forest, avoiding Sloane. Avoiding the embarrassment, the sharp and specific sting of rejection that pulsed in her chest whenever she saw Sloane's face. Max still wasn't sure what had made her do it. At the start of that evening, she'd still hated her and her attitude, her condescension, her picture-perfect life and everything that it held, but there was something underneath all of that, something soft and vulnerable and it had made Max lose every ounce of whatever composure she still had left.

Another angry sigh, and she started the walk back to the lodge's grounds. No poachers, no sign of them at all, and she was starting to think she'd imagined the whole thing, food caches and bears included. A twig snapped under her boot, a pine bough brushed over her shoulder, the waning moon barely visible beyond a sliver of a crescent, leaving the trees in relative darkness, the last vestiges of light perched prettily atop the needled trees, and shining down through the empty branches of others.

The light in reception was still on, much to her surprise. Max checked her watch and raised an eyebrow. What was Orren doing working past midnight? She knocked first, and then opened the door, pushing it in slowly, almost expecting to see him slumped over the desk, asleep on top of some extra paperwork.

"Hey," she said, finding him awake, shuffling through files.

"What are you doing in here so late?" Orren asked, keeping his eyes trained on the files.

"I could ask you the same question."

"Mr. Parker asked me to dredge up records from the past ten to fifteen years."

Max sat in the chair opposite him, leaning forward against her knees. "And the middle of the night is the best time for that?"

"I don't know, Carter, is it the best time for nighttime hikes through the woods?"

"You know why I'm out there."

"And?" He looked up now, prompting her. "What did you find?"

"Nothing."

"You may have to accept that you're not going to find anything out there again, you know. I think you may have scared them off. Or it wasn't poachers at all."

"If it wasn't poachers, then who was it?"

Orren shrugged. "A do-gooder?"

She couldn't tell him it had been dosed with something without admitting to having eaten some of it, so she only returned his shrug. "I doubt it. Why wouldn't someone trying to help stop in at reception, get clearance first?"

"Better to ask forgiveness than permission, I suppose."

"Leaving piles of food in the woods can cause ecological damage, even if it's left with the right intentions. Imagine if I hadn't showed up, if nothing had eaten it, we'd just have caches of rotting fish out there."

"Hardly the worst thing to ever happen in the woods, I'm sure."

"Orren—"

He set the files down on the desk, staring at her purposefully and with such force that it stopped her short. "What's going on with you?" he demanded, setting his glasses down on top of the papers. "All week you've been acting weird."

"I'm not acting weird, I'm just working."

"Not much work lately, yet I never see you."

"I've been in the woods."

"Looking for poachers?" She shrugged again, and he sighed. "Max, I know there's a lot going on, especially this year, but even I can tell that something is off."

"Nothing is off, Orren."

"I think you're a damn liar."

"Think what you want."

He pointed at her. "Aha! See? The old Max would have had some kind of comeback to that, but you just took it."

"I'm just tired."

"From spending all night in the forest?"

"Maybe." Max ran her fingertips over the smooth, polished wood of the desk. "It's hard to comprehend that this will all be gone soon. Crimson Oak will be sold, we'll all be thrown out on our asses, and this place will become another soulless husk of what it once was."

"We may yet stay on." Orren glanced at a form on the wall, detailing which instructor had taught which clients. "You're neck and neck with Sloane, you could still win this."

"I'm not so sure I even want to anymore."

"Now I *know* something is wrong. You were ready to launch her off the side of the mountain a couple of weeks ago."

"I told you, I'm tired." Max leaned back in the chair, feeling the exhaustion pull at her. "Too tired for mind games and competitions. I just want the season to end so I can go back to my crappy little existence back home."

"What happened between you two?"

"Nothing."

"I might be old, Max, but I'm not dead. You went from bitter enemies to... well, whatever you call this. Resignation? Defeat? I didn't see you for nearly three days after the night you went into town to chase after those poachers."

"Just leave it, Orren."

He raised an eyebrow but didn't say anything further, reaching into his desk drawer to produce two individually wrapped cakes shaped like pine trees and frosted white with little dots to represent a garland and ornaments. "Here," he said, tossing one to Max.

"Don't let Bev catch you with those, she'll burn the place down before she lets anyone eat the pre-packaged stuff."

"What Bev doesn't know, won't hurt her." Max unwrapped the cake and took a bite, savoring the almost sickly sweet flavor of vanilla. "Can you ask

Mr. Parker if Sloane can be moved back to the other cabin?"

"The investors are coming back tomorrow, so no."

"You'd think they'd just make up their minds already."

Orren crumpled his cake wrapper, tossing it across the room into the small garbage basket. "I think they just want free time at a lodge where they can pretend to be doing some work, eat free food, and if the snow ever comes back, ski."

"You don't think they want to buy this place after all?" There was a note of too much hopefulness in Max's voice, and she chided herself internally for it.

"No, I think they do, they just want to squeeze every last drop of profitability from it." He gestured to the files laid across his desk before grimacing at the fine layer of crumbs, brushing them into his hand. "It's why I'm in here in the middle of the night, pulling the profit and loss analysis from the past ten years."

"Things would get better if they'd just leave us all alone. They're every-where, all of the time, except the woods." She took another bite, chewed, and swallowed. "It's why I've been up there so much lately."

"Is that the only reason?"

"Yes," Max shot back, too quickly, too confrontational. "Yeah," she said again, more nonchalant. "They ask too many questions."

"They're just trying to get an idea of how this place looks under normal circumstances."

"Nothing about this year is normal."

"No, maybe not." Orren stacked the files, checking the dates on each one as he did. "But what is normal, anyway? Some meaningless baseline that only serves to hinder and abstract."

"Aren't you the philosopher this evening," Max mumbled, finishing her cake.

"You're not the only one who's tired."

Max grimaced. "Sorry. I know you're dealing with all of this, too."

"It would be easier if they'd just give us a straight answer."

"It would be easier if Mr. Parker didn't want to sell the lodge in the first place. What is his problem? There's so much potential for more than just another soulless corporate retreat, but he seems bound and determined for this thing to go through, no matter how much Syndicorp is knocking off the top with every day more that they stay here, inspecting everything, changing the offer over and over again, making amendments for peeling paint, for tow-line maintenance, for refurbishment of the main hall."

"You said yourself that Crimson Oak needs investment."

"Sure, but I didn't mean like *this*."

"It's pointless going through this again, it isn't going to change the reality of the situation, and the reality is that Syndicorp will reach an accord with Mr. Parker and one way or another, Crimson Oak will change."

"Change for the worse, maybe."

"Max—"

She waved him away, the waterproof material of her jacket hissing softly. "I know, I know. You don't have to tell me I'm being too much of a pessimist. I can already feel it in my bones, weighing me down."

"I'm the philosopher, you're the poet."

"Apparently."

A moment passed where the only sounds were the trees blowing gently in the breeze outside, and the incessant countdown of the clock ticking noisily on the wall, every second another one wasted, another moment lost to time, spent on nothing in particular at all, discarded, unused.

Orren looked past her, his gaze settling on the window that looked outside, the crescent moon framed within its pane. "I wish there was another way for all of this to happen."

"I wish a lot of things."

"This year feels different, like there's a river under our feet, and we're moments from being washed out to sea."

"Yeah," Max agreed, nodding, despite the fact he was still staring out over her shoulder. "And there's no way to know when the ice will finally crack. Every day that it doesn't feels stolen, but not in a good way."

"Ominous."

"Yeah."

"Maybe things will get better," Orren said wistfully, finally shifting his stare to meet her face. "Maybe all of this is just a bad dream that we'll wake up from."

"Yeah," Max repeated, cringing at the memory of Sloane pulling away. "Maybe we will."

Chapter 16

Sloane folded her laundry again, every crease perfectly proportioned. She sighed at the empty basket, which gave her nothing more to do. She'd never been so bored in all her life, and that included the hours of waiting for her turn at competitions growing up, standing in the biting cold, her nose going numb as she watched athlete after athlete speed down the side of a mountain. It felt bizarre and pointless, in retrospect. Like she never should have been there in the first place.

The longer she was off the slopes, the more disconnected she became from all of it, from almost an entire lifetime of the same process, training, competing, improving, striving, isolating herself from others to give herself a better chance at winning.

She was tired.

Tired in that bone-deep exhaustion way, the kind that felt like gravity had increased, but only for her, dragging her down closer to the earth just to reclaim her when she finally lost the last scrap of hope from within her. Tired, bored, and frustrated.

There wasn't a moment that passed that she wasn't thinking about that kiss, but she couldn't even let herself crack the surface, not for a moment, not even for a split second, because she'd fall prey to it. She'd be finished. Polar Bears weren't supposed to be with humans, it was too complicated. How were you supposed to hide what you were once every twenty-eight days without suspicion? What would she do if Max discovered her? It didn't bear thinking about, not after what she'd seen happen to others who asked too many questions.

Locked out, ignored, banished, forgotten.

It was easier to never let it start in the first place, but even that was slicing into her like sharp teeth through soft flesh.

She was having a hard enough time dealing with her family without the added complication of Max, of having to plead, and explain, and beg, and in the end it would all be for nothing because no one stayed, anyway. No one ever had. Róisín hadn't, even though that had been ten years ago. Still, the hole she left when she was whisked out to the west coast was palpable.

Sloane could handle being a Polar Bear just fine. She shifted easily, not feeling very sick after like some did, and she enjoyed the freedom, but what sank through her into the core of her being was the ever-present, sucking void of loneliness.

Max hadn't spoken to her in eleven days.

She couldn't blame her, not after what had happened. She probably wouldn't have spoken to herself, either. Sloane laid the laundry in the empty drawer, the one Max had cleaned out for her, wordlessly after what happened in the forest, leaving it open for her to see. She hadn't put anything into it. Not until that moment, and the finality of it was somehow worse than the desperation of possibility.

"Hey," Bev said, knocking on the window. "Mr. Parker wants to see you."

"Ugh, again?" Sloane said, shoving her feet into boots as she opened the door. "What more could he possibly want?"

"He said he wants to help you prepare for the next investor meeting."

"Me?"

"You," Bev confirmed. She searched Sloane's face for something, her head tilted in concern. "You alright?"

"I'm fine."

"You've been hanging around the kitchen for over a week, offering to help chop vegetables and peel potatoes, but you've barely said a word to me."

"I'm just tired, and it's not like there's anything else for me to do out here." Sloane gestured at the slopes, still looking more like late spring than nearly mid-winter. "No clients."

"Still, you don't see Max in here dicing carrots. What's she been doing?

Maybe you should be with her."

"Are you saying you don't want my help?" Sloane bristled at the words, *you should be with her.* If only Bev knew, but she never would.

"No, I'm trying to be nosy and find out where she's been. I was hoping you knew."

"I don't."

"Mr. Parker is waiting in the main hall for you." Bev hesitated, still waiting on the porch. "I know we don't know each other all that well, but given what happened before you wound up out here, I can't help but worry." She shrugged, almost defensively, preparing for Sloane to shoot her down. "It's a mother's intuition. You may not be mine, but I can tell."

"It's nothing."

"I'm not going to pry, but I will say that I know you're lying."

"Sometimes chopping vegetables helps, alright? The... repetition of it, or whatever. It helps you sort out your thoughts."

"I can't argue with that."

Sloane looked out over the slopes again, her brow furrowed. "This season has been a hell of a washout."

"More like green-out."

"It feels like the mountain is telling me I never should have come out here in the first place."

"It does that sometimes," Bev replied, matching her silhouette in staring out over rolling hills in the distance. "But it lies. Just when you think you have this place figured out, it throws you for another loop. It sneaks up on you, and before you know it you're blowing up your entire life just to stay a few more days."

"I'll believe that it's a lie when I get some evidence to support that. So far, it's been nothing but disasters from the bottom up."

Bev gave her a sideways glance and nodded. "I can see why you would feel like that. Come on, I'll walk you over."

"You don't have to do that."

"You're not the only one who's bored, Sloane."

"I thought you'd be busy preparing for the investors to come back tomorrow."

"I'd be busier if you weren't in there doing half my work for me," Bev replied, shooting her a conspiratorial smile. "Not that I'm complaining, but it would be nice to see this place humming. The forecast is nothing but sun as far as the eye can see."

"So much for a snowy Christmas," Sloane muttered. "Isn't that the only reason people book ski lodges over the holidays in the first place?"

"And to avoid their extended families, you can't forget that part," Bev said with a snort. "I won't lie, having to work the holidays has saved me a lot of awkward interactions with my husband's parents."

"You don't mind working over Christmas?"

Bev grinned. "I'm Jewish."

"Oh."

"Mostly non-practicing." Bev started to head towards the main hall, waving for Sloane to follow her. "It works for us. He gets Christmas with his family, and I don't have to argue with his mother over whether the mashed potatoes should have chunks in them." She looked back at Sloane. "For the record, they should *not* have chunks in them."

"Agreed."

"That woman should never have been let loose in a kitchen, but she could be worse, I guess."

Sloane laughed for a moment and stopped, halted by the crisp pinprick of a reminder that she might not have anyone that Christmas or next.

"What's the matter?" Bev asked.

"Nothing, nothing. Rock in my boot," Sloane lied, lifting her foot as though it would prove her point. "Must need new ones."

"Those look pretty new to me."

"Well, you know how it is. Nothing is made like it used to be."

Bev made a small humming sound, partly in agreement, but there was a glint of suspicion layered beneath the tone. "Good luck," she said, depositing Sloane at the door to the main hall. "I'm going to go peel and quarter the potatoes for tomorrow before you slide into the kitchen and do it all."

"I probably won't be long."

"And I peel faster than you. It's been torture watching you remove the skins like you're working in slow motion." Bev elbowed her gently in the ribs. "I'm heading home soon anyway, so I'll see you tomorrow."

"See you tomorrow," Sloane repeated, pulling the heavy door open. It swished closed behind her, and she wiped her boots on the mat before proceeding into the hall, a tinge of sadness that no one else would see the decorations she'd put up. Only Mr. Parker and the investors, and from what she could tell, none of them cared much beyond the check box that it had been done.

"Ms. Hearst, sit down," Mr. Parker said, gesturing to one of the overstuffed sofas in front of the fireplace. There was no fire in it, and the ashes lay cold in the bottom. "I was hoping to better prepare you for the next meeting with investors."

"Prepare me?"

"You seemed nervous last time, jittery. It doesn't send the right message about Crimson Oak."

"I don't particularly enjoy public speaking," she explained. "It isn't my strong suit."

"It's hardly public speaking, there are only seven of us. Besides, from what I understand, you're going to be looking for a new career soon."

Sloane turned to look at him, already repulsed by his tone. "Where did you hear that?"

"People talk."

"I'm fine, thank you."

"Regardless of your intentions after you leave Crimson Oak, I am enlisting you to help me sell this place. It's gone too far, and there's no coming back from the brink. I want to retire, Ms. Hearst, and this lodge isn't going to cut it. Not with the unpredictability of the seasons these past few years."

"As I said last time, I think you would be better served by someone like Orren. He knows this place far better than I ever could. Or Max, even, she—"

"Maxine Carter isn't long for this lodge, Ms. Hearst."

"But we're neck and neck for clients," Sloane refuted. "Depending on what happens, she may well beat me on that count."

"She may, but it's immaterial. What this place needs is someone who really understands the clientèle, who... fits the bill."

"What does that mean?"

"Don't make me specify, you know precisely what I mean. I have hired her back every year because she's passionate and good at the job, but the investors are hoping to curate a different sort of environment at Crimson Oak."

"So they're already calling the shots before you've even signed on the dotted line? That doesn't seem right."

"It's how things work, especially in the absence of other leverage." He gestured hopelessly to the window. "I don't know if you've noticed, but we're barely hanging on by a thread here. Crimson Oak's best chance is this deal."

"Or?"

"Or it lays empty and I go bankrupt next year. I've already put everything I had into this place. It was my mother's, and my grandmother's before her, but they always put every cent they made back into the lodge. It didn't leave much."

"I don't know how much help I can be," Sloane said, tracing an old water stain on the coffee table in front of her. "I've never had a head for business."

"That's why you're here now, so we can go over everything in excruciating detail. The better prepared you are—the better prepared we both are—the more likely this place will live on in some respect, even if it's not really what I wanted."

Sloane glanced at the door, willing Max to appear and save her from it, but she didn't, because Sloane had made it clear she wanted nothing to do with her. "I'd always assumed you were hoping for investors," she said.

"Not in the beginning, but things are becoming harder and harder to manage. We shortened the seasons first, we allocated cabins to full-time staff only to save on energy bills and space, we cut programs that didn't perform as well as we'd hoped, we've tried everything, but it's barely made a dent in what we need to keep this place alive."

"But Orren—"

"Orren Ralt is a good man, but investors don't want to see good men, they want to see promise and tangible proof of it. The same way that people paint all the walls white before they sell a house, we have to make Crimson Oak look like it holds endless appeal and promise." He sighed, opening a notebook. "Do you understand?"

Sloane glanced back at him, chewing the inside of her cheek. "Yes," she replied, resigned, "I understand."

Chapter 17

Max sat at the top of the ski-tow line, running her fingers through parched grass. The landscape was all wrong, the deciduous trees bare for winter but grass spread across the slope and beyond over the hills like a bad omen. A sign that things were getting worse, if that was even possible anymore. How much worse could things really get, now that she had no prospects, no place of her own at Crimson Oak or back home, no real friends outside the job she was probably about to lose, no possibility of getting where she wanted to be in life?

It was bleak, and so was the scene in front of her. She sighed, leaning back on the grass, letting the brittle blades scratch at her neck because there was no point in fighting them, just like there was no point in fighting the power of Syndicorp. The ones with the money were always the ones who won, who walked away with the prize, who stole the trophies and locked them away for safekeeping. People like Max never really had a chance.

The sun was starting to set over the hills draped at the horizon, sinking lower and lower, taking the last vestiges of daylight with it. She checked her watch and sighed. Four in the afternoon. Only a few days from the solstice, the shortest day of the year, and again she'd be walking through the woods looking for poachers who had apparently vanished. It didn't make any sense—why spend all that money on premium bait just to abandon it? Most poachers weren't discouraged by pursuit, and if it was the same ones from years ago, they definitely hadn't been. Perhaps the threat of being caught again was enough to scare them away, but she doubted it.

Something felt off at Crimson Oak, and it wasn't the pack of investors that had reappeared that afternoon, or the fact that Sloane had barely said anything to her after the kiss, or the looming knowledge that she was about to lose the only good job she'd ever had, it was something in the woods, something secret and protected, and it was eating at her mind like poison.

The Wolf in her always had been good at detecting things, which was why she still blamed herself for what had happened years back. Something had nagged at her, and she'd ignored it, and wolves died as a result of her complacency. There weren't many left in that part of the country, and they'd died on her watch, and the guilt followed her around, ever-present, even when she was two hundred miles and months away from Crimson Oak.

She stood, brushing the dirt and debris from her hips and back, flicking on the flashlight in the encroaching darkness. Once again, she entered the trail, ready to find evidence, ready to flush out whatever was hiding in there.

Once again, she found nothing, and it had been an hour wasted, not that she had much else to do while the slopes were dry. The investors were all holed up in the lodge, except for the development team, who'd taken over the remaining staff cabins. The site was far from full, but it still carried a particular feeling of specific emptiness, like the liminality of an airport or a gas station, like she was just passing through despite the fact she'd spent months there every year for over a decade.

The wrongness of it continued to settle beneath her skin, and it made her uneasy, jittery, energized in that same way as before a strong shift. It was the wrong time of the lunar cycle for that, and her other cycle had only just finished. There was no reason for the prickled sensation of indefinable glitch of self that pulled at her, but it dragged at her nonetheless. Maybe it was all of it, all at once that was making her feel that way. Maybe it was none of it, and she was just being paranoid.

* * *

When Max awoke the next morning, it was to an eerie silence, devoid of the usual quiet noise of Crimson Oak. There were no crows calling from the distant trees, no quiet chatter of the investors as they pored over every inch of the lodge, no cars softly rumbling along the street below the mountain. She sat up, rubbing her eyes, surprised at the lack of bright, demanding sunlight through the thin curtains.

She planted her feet on the ground, quietly groaning as she greeted what might be her last day on the mountain. Maybe the last day ever, and she still hadn't uncovered the mystery of what was going on in the woods, far from the trails. Now, she likely never would, and those poachers would be left to do whatever they wanted for two seasons, until the corporate buyers brought in security the next year.

Pulling back the curtain, she gave a quiet gasp. The earth was covered in thick, wet snow, and it was still falling fast from the sky. Relief surged in her chest, but it was quickly followed by fear. The snow was already over a foot deep and still coming. "Shit," she murmured, trying to push open the door.

"What's wrong?" Sloane mumbled from the top bunk.

"We're snowed in."

"Snow?"

"Yeah, and lots of it." Max frowned at the outside, holding the curtain aside so that Sloane could see. "Too much, too fast."

"The access road—"

"That will be blocked, if I had to guess, and if I had to make a second guess, it would be that these investors aren't going to be thrilled to be stuck up here."

"Can we get out?"

"Maybe." Max tried the door again, throwing her weight into it. It creaked, opening just wide enough for one person to fit, if they turned sideways. "Kind of."

"What about the slopes?"

"I don't know, you can't see anything through this snow."

"Whiteout?"

Max nodded. "Definitely."

"Damn." Sloane jumped down from the top bunk, landing heavy on her feet, solid and planted. "We should see if anyone needs us."

"I wonder if Bev managed to get in before it hit."

"Not judging by the amount of snow, she didn't. It must have started late last night.

Max shook her head. "I didn't see anything when I was out there, barely even a cloud. The forecast didn't call for this either, it's like it's a freak storm."

"You know how it is these days, these storms can crop up out of nowhere."

"Yeah, but it can't be good, not long term." Max rubbed her arms, the chill of the snow seeping under the door like tendrils. "The temperature certainly dropped."

"Probably lake-effect snow, then."

"Undoubtedly."

"Suit up? We can see about getting the access road cleared, maybe."

"I'll join you." Max tugged on a pair of thick long underwear, savoring the gentle texture of the waffle stitch pattern before covering them with two more layers. It was nice to have Sloane talking to her again, but mentioning that felt like she might break the spell the snow had laid on the lodge, covering the vague notion that something was wrong with a visible problem that needed attention right away. "At least any poachers won't be able to make it up those back paths, not in these conditions."

"Small mercies."

"I haven't, uh—found anything out there. So far. In the woods."

Sloane glanced over her shoulder as she pulled on her snow pants over the insulated layers. "Maybe that's the end of it, then?" she suggested.

"I don't think so, there's something I'm missing. Something that feels off about Crimson Oak this year."

"Off?" Sloane asked, now focusing on tying the laces of her fur-lined boots. "Off how?"

"I don't know, just... off. Like there's something hiding, something I can't quite figure out."

"Maybe the woods are haunted."

"Wrong season for that, Hearst, and we stopped the haunted hay rides years ago."

"Why?"

"Oh, you know. Funding. It's always funding, always tightening the belt, never loosening it. The less attention Parker paid it, the less popular it got, until finally it wasn't earning its keep, so to speak." Max shrugged. "So they stopped."

"I hope you aren't planning on going into the woods today, not with this weather."

"It depends on whether there might be poachers in there or not." Max tied a double knot in her own boot laces, pulling them tight to secure them and tucking the excess beneath the tongue. "First, we should find Orren. The man hates blizzards."

"At a ski lodge?"

"At a winter sports lodge, and yes, he prefers the delicate predictability of a reliable weather forecast. Given he's the one who has to deal with the phones that ring off the hook every time this happens, I can't blame him."

"Every time?"

"Sort of. Most times we at least get a day or two of warning before it hits. This time, we've all been smacked by it without so much as a whisper on the nightly reports."

"Max?" Orren called through the door. "Max, open up, you won't believe—"

She pushed open the door again, wedging her boot in the gap to keep it open. "I saw the snow. I know."

"You're awake."

"We both are, we were about to come find you. Phones ringing?"

Orren shook his head. "Phones are out."

"Damn."

"Phones are out and half the electricity. We're running on generators now, but it only feeds the main hall and the lodge."

Max flipped the switch on the wall, frowning when nothing happened. "Looks like it. What now?"

"Hunker down and wait for the lines to come back up, but in the meantime, we have a pack of investors to keep happy," Orren said. "And Mr. Parker isn't on site."

"Did he drive home last night?"

"As far as I know. But he left a voicemail on the reservations system about pulling more data sheets, and that was after midnight, so we can assume he got home okay. But until he's back, we're all this place has."

"What do we need?" Sloane asked, standing behind Max now, standing so close that Max couldn't help but tense at her proximity. "Bev?"

"Her car isn't in the parking lot, and she's local so let's run on the assumption that she can't make it in, either."

"I can prep some food, if—"

"Finally!" one of the investors yelled from the porch of the kitchen, already marching over to them in attire that was not conducive to the weather. "I've been looking everywhere for someone who works here. Is this place staffed by ghosts?"

"What do you need, sir?" Orren asked. "We'll be getting food prepared as soon as we—"

"Lyons is missing."

"Lyons?" Max asked. "Walter Lyons, the head of Winter Sports Magazine? He's an investor?"

"He has a vested interest, if that's what you mean. He's missing. Went out this morning when he saw the snow, said he wanted to check out the slopes, and no one has seen him since. His room is empty."

Max exchanged a look with Orren, and then turned to Sloane. "Do you think there's a chance he tried to go skiing?"

"Maybe. You need to call mountain rescue, get someone out here right away!"

"Listen, Mr.—" Max shrugged at him. "I don't know your name."

"Jim. Osset."

"Mr. Osset, the phone lines are down, along with the power. The lodge and the main hall are running on generators, but that won't last forever and this snow has no signs of stopping. We can't call mountain rescue, and to walk into town would take hours in this snow, not to mention it's dangerous. The best thing you can do is to let us handle it." She glanced back at Sloane again, and was startled to see her already geared up. "That was fast."

"Let's go, Carter," she said. "First we check the slopes. Get your board."

"I'll manage the tow-line to pull you back up," Orren announced, rubbing his hands together to fight against the settling cold. "Mr. Osset, we'll do our best, but I need you to go back to the lodge and tell everyone else to stay put. We can't have more people getting lost out here, even *we* will have a hard time, and we know this place like the back of our hands."

Jim Osset nodded, pulling his wool peacoat tight around himself. "I'll tell them. You know, this is why I never took up skiing."

"And yet, you're here trying to buy out a ski lodge," Max replied, shaking her head. "No wonder this deal is—"

Orren cleared his throat loudly, and Max stopped herself, pulling a tight-fitting knitted hat over her head. "Anyway, Hearst and I will check the slopes first, and then the mountain, if we don't find him." She grabbed her thick parka from the hook on the back of the door, zipping it close around herself. "Orren, grab the controls. Let's find Mr. Lyons."

Chapter 18

"You take this one, I'll take the bunny slope," Sloane said, clipping into her skis. "That way I can do a turnaround down there and check the couple of trails at the foot of the mountain."

"And here I thought you'd fight me for the main slope," Max said, pulling the straps tight across her boots. "But that sounds like a plan."

"You're more familiar with the woods, it only makes sense that you should have that side. Besides, I don't need to prove anything to you, you've already seen me ski."

"I think you might have fought me if this happened the day you arrived."

Sloane straightened, digging her poles into wet snow. "The day I arrived, I was still reeling from dropping out of nationals qualifiers. I was defensive and rude, and I don't think it was a good demonstration of who I really am." She chewed the inside of her cheek as she pushed to the crest of the small slope. "And for that, I am sorry."

Without waiting for a reply, she pushed herself over the edge of the slope, weaving from side to side, scanning the snow for any indentations that might indicate tracks, but with the snow falling so heavy and so fast, there was nothing to find, even if the missing investor had decided to go for an early morning ski session.

Sloane twisted, coming to a stop at the bottom of the small hill. She peered past the tree line into the small thicket, knowing it was beset on all sides by fencing there, to keep people away from the drastic drop on the other side. With a sick feeling in the pit of her stomach, she pressed into the trees, pushing herself along on skis. It would have been better with cross-country skis, but she didn't have hers with her, and the lodge didn't have any on site. A shame, as there would be some stunning tracks up on the other side of the mountain if they had.

She laid a hand against half-frozen bark, pushing herself deeper into the woods. There was no sign anyone had been there, no tracks or snapped twigs, and with the relative shelter of the pine branches overhead, the snow was thinner on the ground there and easier to read. Nothing. Breathing a sigh of relief, she went back the way she came, just in time to see Max snowboarding to the bottom of the main slope, slowly weaving a snakelike trail in the snow as she peered into the forest. Sloane raised her poles over her head in the shape of an X to communicate she hadn't found Lyons.

Max waved her over with a wide gesture, and Sloane followed, dragging through the heavy, wet snow until she reached the base of the ski-lift. "Did you find anything?" Sloane asked, looking up the hill to see if Orren was waiting in the booth yet.

"No. I'm not so sure he was out here."

"Me neither. Hard to tell for sure with how fast and heavy this stuff is falling, but he's a seasoned skier, I don't think he would do something like that, especially without the lift running. What do you think?"

"I never met him, not really, but it would be strange if he did that." Sloane waved up to Orren, who waved back as the cables began to shift, pulling the chairs down towards them. "How about the woods?"

"I didn't see anything, but it might be an idea to get a better look from up there, where the trailhead starts."

"Why would he go hiking in a blizzard?" Sloane asked, shaking her head. "That's just asking for trouble."

"Only if you don't know where you're going."

"Right, which he doesn't. Had he even ever been here before all this talk of deals started with Syndicorp?"

Max sighed. "Not as far as I know." She looked up at the greying sky and frowned. "There's no sign that this is stopping any time soon, and if I know Bear Mountain, the temperatures are going to start dropping not long after noon. What time is it now?"

"Eleven."

"We don't have much time, then."

Sloane turned, preparing for the chair to hook behind her knees, and Max did the same, unhooking one of her boots from the board so that she could sit properly. Sloane transferred her poles into one hand as the chair grabbed them, pulling the safety bar down over them both. "Where do we start?"

"The main trails, I'd guess, but there are all those side trails that haven't been cleared in at least a year, maybe longer. If he lost the trail in the snow, he could be anywhere on the mountain."

The lift brought them to the top, where they both dismounted in unison. "Orren," Sloane called, her hands cupped around her mouth. "Any word on mountain rescue? Or the phones?"

"Nothing," he replied with an apologetic shrug. "I'm guessing we won't have either until at least tomorrow."

"We need to find that man, or he's going to freeze out here tonight," Max said, unhooking her other boot. "I hope you have actual winter hiking boots, and not just those fancy ski boots you're wearing."

"Of course I have winter hiking boots, what do you think I am, an animal?" Sloane asked, holding a hand over her chest in mock annoyance. "Yes, they're in the cabin. Are yours?"

"By the foot of the beds."

"I'll get them."

"You don't have to—"

"You and Orren know Crimson Oak better than any of the rest of us. Formulate a plan in the ninety seconds it's going to take me to get them and come back, okay?"

Max tilted her head, staring, and then nodded. "Okay."

"Good." Sloane unclipped from her skis, leaving them leaning against the control booth. "In case I need them again," she explained as she walked away.

Crisis or no, it was nice that Max was talking to her again. At least it was more substantial than asking if she was done with the bathroom, or whether she wanted to do laundry first or second when it was their slot. Sloane exhaled, and her breath curled into smoky ribbons. Max was right about the temperatures starting to drop, and now some missing hiker had multiple problems. Hypothermia, dehydration, exposure, or wolves. Any of them, enough to at least cause a hospital stay. The wolf she'd seen on the mountain hadn't seemed aggressive, but rabies could take hold in just a few short days. There was no telling what it might have, living in the woods alone like it did.

She pushed into the cabin, immediately locating both pairs of boots. She tugged her own on, not even stopping to tighten the laces, and pulling Max's from beneath her bottom bunk. Once again into the increasingly frigid blizzard, she tugged her goggles over her eyes to protect against the blowing snow that continued to collect on her eyelashes.

"Here," she said, tossing the boots to Max. She put her own ski boots into the control shed, next to her skis. "Orren, what's the plan?"

"You and Max are going to hike the main trail, hopefully you find him there. I'm really hoping he didn't get ambitious or lost, although either is entirely possible." He stopped the tow-line and climbed out of the booth, tightening the scarf around his neck. "That Jim Osset said that he wasn't sure how long Lyons had been gone for. For all we know, he was out as soon as the blizzard started early this morning. We could be looking at hours of exposure already."

"And there's no chance that Lyons is somewhere on the main site? He's not poking around the kitchen, or hiding in some nook in the main hall?"

Orren shook his head. "I double and triple checked, and with the phone lines out and no cell service up here, I can't imagine he was able to get a taxi to take him to the airport or anything like that."

"Please, there's one taxi here, and it runs approximately two days a week for three hours," Max griped. "No, he must be on the mountain." She sighed angrily. "Damn it."

"Let's get a move on, you lead," Sloane said, pulling her insulated mittens on over her hands. "The sooner we find Lyons, the better."

"Come on, Hearst, follow up," Max said, already making long strides towards the trail head. Despite the snow and the frigid air, she wasn't even winded. Sloane couldn't help but be impressed.

"I hope the phones come back up soon, then we can call mountain rescue."

"I'd be surprised if we'd even see them within two days," Max called back to her, ducking under branches heavy and laden with snow, hanging lower to the ground than usual. "Not many mountains up this way."

"Emergency services, then, someone might be able to find him."

"There's no way a helicopter can run in this weather, and the state police will be busy with road accidents and heck knows what else."

"I guess it's up to us, then." Sloane swallowed hard. Even saying the words aloud made the pit in her stomach deepen, allowing more anxiety in the form of bile to rush in. "No pressure."

"I thought you'd be used to high-pressure environments."

"Not like this. Not when lives are on the line."

Max looked back at her, a tuft of dark hair escaping from beneath the neon knit hat she was wearing. "We can do this."

"We can." Sloane squared her shoulders and nodded. "You're right. We can do this."

"Hard to imagine that Parker doesn't even know what's going on up here. He's totally out of the loop."

"I think Orren is going to try hiking to the bottom of the mountain to get a signal to call, but there's no telling how helpful that will be. It's not like Mr. Parker will be able to magically solve the problems, and it's not as though calling emergency services will mean they make it out here in time."

"And they don't know the mountain like you do."

"That too." Max held a pine bough aside, waiting for Sloane to pass before she released it, sending an extra spray of snow to shake down across the undulating mounds on the wet forest floor. "I just wish we had some clue of where he could have gone."

"I guess this is the best place to start." Their own footprints were already being filled with more snow, and Sloane kicked at a small drift. "It's going to be hard to track anyone, the way this snow is still coming down."

"And the branches snapping because they're so weighed down are obscuring the trail as well. Why would he go out in a blizzard? You'd think that someone so intimately familiar with the dangers would know better."

Sloane grimaced, stepping over a half-rotted tree trunk that blocked the invisible path. "I've seen more than a few overconfident skiers get in over their heads when things like this happen. They all think that disasters only happen to other people, and that it hasn't happened to them because of their skill and knowledge." She dodged a low-hanging branch that Max had missed, too short to notice. "The thing is, winding up lost on a mountain could happen to any of us."

"I hope he doesn't make the same mistake again."

"You might be surprised by the number of people that do."

"Not surprised, just disappointed."

"Ouch."

Max snorted a laugh, and the sound was strangely deadened by all the wet snow surrounding them. "What's the matter, can't handle disappointing others?"

"Not really, no."

"You should get used to it, it's very freeing to decide you no longer care about what other people think."

"Easier when they're not your family."

"True enough." Max glanced back at her, an eyebrow raised. "Family isn't everything."

"It's a lot, though."

"Sure, but look how many people are stumbling around their own existence, damaged and broken and completely crushed by their families." Max shrugged, turning back to face the unwalked trail ahead of them. "When was the last time you had a conversation with any of them that improved your day?"

Sloane laughed before she even had much time to think about it. "Never."

"Then you, Sloane Hearst, deserve better."

"Do I?"

"Yeah." Max smacked a branch, and it sprang upwards, relieved of the snow's weight. "We all deserve better."

For a moment, or maybe even three, the only sound was that of their boots crunching against the snow. Despite how it continued to fall, the plummeting temperatures had already begun to form a crust across the top, easily destroyed but present nonetheless.

"Any ideas where he went?" Sloane asked. "I don't see anything."

"I don't either, but there's not that many places he could have gone." The radio at Max's hip buzzed unpleasantly, and she flinched as she unclipped it. "Orren?"

"Yeah," the radio fuzzed. "No cell service at the bottom, snow must have taken out a tower."

"Damn."

"Any luck?" he asked, and his earnest, hopeful tone was palpable even through the thick static.

"No, not yet. We're still looking."

"It's almost two, it's not long before it starts to get dark. Once that happens..." he trailed off, but the implication was apparent.

Max sighed. "I know. You don't have to tell me, we're doing our best." She waited a moment, and then added, "over and out."

"Too bad we don't have dogs up here, maybe that would help," Sloane mused aloud. What she was really thinking was that she'd be much more useful as a Bear than as a human, feeble and too affected by temperatures and environments. Weak and unable to help, the same as she always had been. But it was almost halfway through the lunar cycle, and the moon would only be a sliver, and besides, the worst thing she could do would be to shift before emergency services showed up.

"Dogs," Max repeated.

"You know, to help track down Lyons."

"No, I know what you meant. I was just thinking."

"About?"

"About what you said, Hearst, come on, keep up."

Sloane followed behind, rolling her eyes. "Why, do you keep a pack of hounds up your sleeve?"

"I wish that was the case."

"We're almost looped back to the trail head now, aren't we?"

"And no sign of him," Max confirmed. "What a disaster. He could be anywhere, if he's not on this trail."

"What are the odds he left the trail back here, went wandering deeper into the woods?"

"It's not impossible."

"Where did you find those caches?" Sloane asked.

"He can't have been one of the poachers."

"I just meant if there are any attractive spots around here, like a shelter, or a large tree, or—" Sloane stopped dead in her tracks. "What if he took one of the back trails down the mountain?" She laid a hand on Max's shoulder as she bent to examine one spot where the trail forked. "You mentioned that's how you thought the poachers were getting up here."

"There are at least twelve different back trails from the base, there's no way we'd be able to hike them all before sundown."

"We could split up, cover twice as much ground."

"That's a terrible idea, especially in this weather."

Sloane nodded at the sky. "It's starting to lighten up. Our problem now is the cold, and how I'm betting he's not exactly dressed for the weather."

"I don't like it. What if you get lost?"

"I won't get lost. I have a very keen sense of direction."

"Sloane—"

"He could die if we don't find him. No, not could, will, especially if these temperatures continue to nosedive. If we don't split up, I don't want to know what we'll find in the morning."

Max hesitated, bracing herself against the trunk of a tree. "If we were to lose you too... that's not a loss I am prepared to sacrifice."

"Oh." It was all Sloane could say, and the syllable nearly exploded in her mind, a spectacular display of awkwardness and ineptitude.

"Take this spare flashlight, then," Max added, her tone a bit harsher now. "Can't have you walking around in the dark all night."

"Thanks."

"We don't have a spare radio, but listen, if you get lost. If for even one moment you're not sure where you are, or you think you might have taken a wrong turn, just try to head down the mountain. If you're not back at the trail head in three hours, I'll hike down to the base and find you. It will suck walking back up to the lodge, so try not to do that."

"I'll do my best."

Three hours, Sloane, not one minute more."

"I hear you."

Max tossed her the flashlight, giving her a look that was between concern and something else she couldn't quite place. "I mean it."

"I won't be late." Sloane slid the flashlight into her pocket, despite knowing she wasn't going to be using it. "What if you find him first?"

"Orren has a flare gun at the lift booth, we'll fire two if we find Lyons. Keep your eyes on the sky." Max folded her arms over her chest, more a protective gesture than a hostile one. "Though given all that knowledge you have about the stars, it seems like you already do."

"Lots of cloud cover today, but it might be clearing. At least if the snow stops, the plows can start on the roads."

"It will still be hours, even half a day before they get out this far."

"Better than nothing."

"Yeah."

Sloane hesitated, knowing that she had to leave to look for Lyons, but wishing she could stay, to tell her why she pulled away, to try to explain it, but it was impossible, and there was no way back from where they'd been. "Three hours, then."

"On the dot."

"I'll start on the easternmost trail and hike back and forth until I find something."

"We'd better hope that one of us does. I'm sure someone dying of exposure on the mountain isn't quite the publicity that Mr. Parker is hoping for."

Sloane winced at the comment, reminded of why she was out there in the first place. She nodded, zipping her pockets closed and pulling her hood up over her insulated hat. A show, a performance, because she'd be out of it sooner rather than later, and damn the consequences. She'd be fine. She'd *probably* be fine.

"Are you okay? You're just standing there."

"Yeah. Thinking. Okay, I'm going now." Sloane turned on her heel, marching off into the woods. As soon as she was out of Max's line of sight, she changed track, heading for the northern face of the mountain. She'd check the eastern trails eventually, but for what she was planning, she needed total seclusion.

Chapter 19

Max scoured the woods for an hour and a half before the real cold set in. She longed for the warmth of a Wolfish fur coat, bundled inside her parka and shivering. The cold didn't usually bother her much, but the temperature was plummeting, and had gone from a manageable just below freezing to well within a problem zone, especially if Lyons had been out there since the morning. They were running out of time.

No word from Sloane was a bad sign, too. Max had been sure she'd find him on the eastward trails and drag him back to the lodge unharmed, but there had been no radio calls, no sign of him or of Sloane. Dread slipped down into Max's stomach at the realization that Sloane could be lost or hurt, or waiting at the bottom of the mountain after getting turned around. She didn't know Bear Mountain very well at all, and it was entirely possible she'd lost the marked trail beneath the snow.

Icicles formed across previously barren branches, dripping down into tiny spears, miniature javelins poised and waiting. The forest seemed different now that she was fighting against it, angrily thrashing through ice-frosted snow to keep it from claiming a life. Lyons had been missing for half a day, and the sun had now disappeared behind the horizon. Without much moonlight, every pine tree looked like a threat with its dancing shadows, and every wispy cloud was a death sentence as it passed over what little light there was.

Max retraced her steps for a third time, still calling out his name, still getting no response beyond the quiet whistling of wind through branches. She crossed her own path four times over, walking between trails in case he'd gotten lost, but there was nothing, no sign of him, and panic started to bloom in her chest. She'd been so sure they'd find him, but it was starting to look increasingly unlikely.

She glared up at the slivered moon, cursing it for not being full. She'd never been able to summon the Wolf without it, not even when she'd tried, not even when she'd been so angry that she thought she might burst from it, not even when the urge to run free among the trees was so strong that it itched beneath her skin.

With one last glance over her shoulder, she headed for the eastern trails. At least there she could link up with Sloane and find out where she'd covered, and make a plan to tackle the rest. If Lyons was alive, he may not be conscious by now, unable to reply to their calls. She edged past a fallen tree, one that had been there at least ten years. She remembered the season it fell, struck down by a late autumn lightning storm. The charred wood remained on the forest floor like an omen from above.

She'd spent a good amount of time in her life swearing at the sky, either because the moon was too full or not full enough and the lack of control was maddening at times. To be so completely beholden to it, with no recourse, felt more like a curse than a gift, and that's how her family had treated it, too. It wasn't unheard of in her family—her great aunt Rosa had it too—but it was rare, and no one knew what to do with her once she started shifting. Gradually, she pulled away, and they let her, and that was that.

The trailhead for the easternmost path was marked with orange posts hammered into the frozen, rocky ground, the soil up there poor in nutrients but it was good enough for trees, at least. Max started down the trail, now calling out for Lyons and Sloane. Her boot snagged on a root, and she stumbled, throwing her hands out in front of her for balance. She hit the ground with a heavy thud, her palms scraping against the rocks beneath the snow, a scraping sting that jarred her.

"Sloane!" she shouted again, angrier this time. Where the hell was she? It was possible she'd moved on to another trail already, but she'd have to be covering some serious ground to be so far as to not hear her voice, carried on the wind. Sound traveled far up on the mountain, even despite the trees.

Max squinted into the darkness, willing herself to see more, to see further, to be less limited by her feeble human eyesight. Something like a footprint snagged her attention, and she bent with her flashlight to examine it. Whatever it was, it was huge, larger than anything she'd ever seen up there before.

Her breath caught in her throat, ragged with apprehension. As far as she knew, there were no more bears on Bear Mountain, they'd all been moved on decades before she'd even started working there. Not even Orren remembered there being bears, not even Mr. Parker. It had turned into a local joke, having a mountain named for something that had abandoned it long ago.

If there were bears on the mountain, bears that weren't hibernating, that had been pulled from it too early with the warm spell of temperatures they'd had over recent weeks, then Lyons and Sloane were both in even more danger. The night was one thing, the cold was another, but adding in a fierce predator was worry enough to force the air from her chest in panic.

She had to get back to Orren, to tell him that something was out there. She shouted Sloane's name again, desperate this time, pleading with her to answer because the longer she stayed silent, the more Max became convinced that there was a terrible reason she hadn't found either of them yet. She should have known not to let Sloane go off by herself, she should have insisted they stay together, but now it was too late, and too dark, and even if she raised the alarm it would take far too long to get help.

Max took three more steps along the path, following the tracks of whatever was out there. It looked like a bear's tracks, but huge, amplified, much larger than any black bear's should be in the Midwest. It was like a strange compulsion to keep following, as though it wasn't going to lead to a huge beast that would only add her to the menu alongside the others. It would have to be the biggest black bear in existence. Grizzlies had no business there, they were hundreds of miles away.

What if the vision of the bear that night she found the first cache hadn't been a hallucination at all?

The thought slammed into her with a gale force, and she stumbled against it. Had there been a bear out there all along? Is that what the poachers were hunting? She'd thought she knew the mountain, every inch of it, every fallen tree and snapped branch and tiny eddy where the river hesitated along the banks, but she was being forced to admit that maybe she hadn't known anything at all.

That she'd come face to face with death, and convinced herself it was a mirage.

Max swallowed hard, stepping further down the trail, each step emitting a small crunch, and she resented herself for it. The frosted snow was noisy but frustratingly unavoidable, even beneath the shelter of the pine trees. The blizzard had come so fast, and with so much strength, that every inch of the mountain was covered with it and crusted over in the frigid temperatures.

"Sloane?" she asked, quieter this time despite knowing that noise was one of the best ways to ward off a bear. She cursed herself for not bringing bear spray, but then, why would she? Bears weren't in those parts, not anymore.

Or so she'd thought.

A quiet snuffle ahead sent adrenaline shooting through her veins. Hands shaking, she raised the beam of the flashlight and stared, unable to process what she was seeing.

An enormous, hulking polar bear, dragging an unconscious Lyons. The bear looked as startled as she felt, and the flashlight fell to the ground.

"Hey!" Max shouted, waving her arms over her head. "Don't come near me!" Shout at black bears, play dead with grizzlies, but polar bears were another story. Really, she was dead already. There would be no outrunning it, not without—she winced against the sharp pain in her side, bending double. She wasn't sure whether she should be terrified or grateful as the Wolf pulled herself to the forefront, bending Max to her will.

Tangled in her clothes, she panicked, tearing at the parka with teeth and claws as she struggled to get free, to run, to escape. She'd never shifted outside a full moon but it was different, painful, uncomfortable like wearing a shirt with an itchy tag but if there were a million tags, all at once, scraping along your skin like crushed glass.

The bear hadn't moved. It stayed, staring, as though it was as surprised as she was. Lyons was still in its grip, but as Max's snout lengthened, she still couldn't smell any blood. Was he dead already? No, she could sense that he wasn't, but he was in trouble, and not just from the bear.

Max tore herself free from the remains of her clothing, turning tail and running back for camp. The bear made a strange, guttural roar, and when she turned back, she stopped. The bear was sitting back on its haunches, watching with a tilted head. Was it scared of her? Confused to see a wolf emerge from human skin? The bear's black eyes had something strangely human about them, and something about the way it nudged Lyons forward to lean him against a tree gave Max pause.

She stared, and the bear stared.

For a long time, neither of them blinked.

She should have known, really, but she hadn't.

She'd spent so many years apart from any others that she'd almost forgotten she wasn't the only one. The adrenaline fading, she could feel the Wolf retreat, and moment by moment she shifted back, shivering in the snow, grasping for her torn clothes and pulling them on. She stood, still staring, keeping her eyes on the Bear as she bent to loosen her boot laces to put them back on.

The Bear turned her head towards a tree, where a small duffel bag hung from a low branch. Max nodded, taking it down. She tossed the bag into the darkness of the trees and turned to Lyons as the Bear went after the bag. "Sir?" she said, checking his pulse. Weak, but still there. He was breathing at least, but he was likely severely hypothermic. "Sir, we're going to get you back to the lodge. You need medical attention."

Max snapped some instant heat packs and slipped them into his coat. It wasn't much, but every little bit helped.

When Sloane stepped out of the trees, three twigs sticking out of her usually neat braid, Max almost laughed. "I thought I was a goner."

"How did you know?"

"I just knew."

Sloane glanced at Lyons. "It's probably a good thing he's unconscious."

"Even if he isn't, no one is going to believe that."

"You should radio Orren."

Max nodded, reaching for the radio with one hand and helping to lift Lyons with the other. "Orren, come in Orren."

"Max?"

"We've got him. Sloane found him, and I found her, and we're headed back."

"I can meet you at the trailhead with a snowmobile."

"In ten. Over and out."

Between the two of them, they lifted, dragged, and carried Lyons out of the woods. Neither of them said a word, but Max's heart clenched in her chest every time she made accidental eye contact with Sloane. She was a Bear. A damned Polar Bear, and she hadn't known. How hadn't she figured it out sooner?

"Load him onto the sled," Orren said, waiting at the tree line. "Bev made it up, she brought the paramedics with her."

"Good, he's going to need them," Sloane said, strapping him to the sled.

"What happened to you?" Orren asked, staring at Max. "You look like you got attacked."

"Disagreement with some old thorn bushes back there."

"Thorn bushes."

"Yeah, Orren, thorns. What else would it be? We're clearly fine. Go! We'll hike back to the main hall."

He gave her a strange look, but revved the engine and headed back towards the lodge, the sled in tow with Lyons.

"So," Sloane said after a long moment.

"So," Max repeated.

"They were my food caches in the woods, there weren't any poachers."

"Yeah, I did manage to figure that one out." Max gave her a sideways glance. "How long have you known?"

"That there were no poachers? Only when you mentioned that the evidence was just the caches."

"You didn't say anything."

Sloane breathed out a quiet laugh. "What could I have said? I didn't know you were a Wolf until you shifted in front of me."

"Sorry about that."

"No, don't be sorry, it's..." Sloane trailed off, shaking her head. "It's kind of amazing. I've never met a Wolf."

"I've never met a Bear."

"That you know of."

Max nodded, her eyes following the trail of the snowmobile. "How did you find him?"

"I knew I'd never find him without shifting." Sloane tapped the end of her nose, pink in the frosty air. "Bears have a much better sense of smell than humans or Wolves."

"I don't know about that."

"It's true, and don't argue with me."

"Alright." Max glanced at her again, and swallowed hard. "I've never shifted outside a full moon before."

"Never?"

"Nope. Never been able to. Seems like the key for me is thinking I'm about to die."

Sloane nodded. "I've heard that can be the case for some Weres."

"Do you do this often? Shifting outside the cycle?"

"No. Trust me, you'll know why in about an hour or so."

Max groaned. "So what you're telling me is that the feeling of being right before a bad flu, that's because of the shift?"

"Mhmm."

"At least you found him."

"*We* found him. It was taking too long to drag him back on my own, but I would have been even slower as, well, as me."

"Maybe we have a future in search and rescue, what do you think?" Max asked quietly, half joking, but all of her wanting to fix whatever she'd broken between them.

"I don't know if I could deal with the stress."

"What now?"

"I guess we head back, wait to hear something. If Bev made it up, she'll need help in the kitchen."

"Do you think that's the best idea right now, with how we're feeling? Or rather, about to feel?"

Sloane started walking towards the lodge, wrapping her arms tight around herself. "I bet if we're nice, we can get hold of some soup and some juice, and I promise that makes a big difference."

"Wait—hang on, I—" Max jogged through the heavy snow to keep up, but stopped short when words tangled in her mouth.

"What's wrong?"

"Nothing, I—" Max's mouth opened and closed soundlessly, and she shook her head. "Nothing, it's nothing. Let's go." She wanted to ask why Sloane pulled away, why she had barely spoken to her in eleven—twelve days, and if it was just that she was a Polar Bear, then surely that didn't matter as much as it did before, now that she knew, but maybe Sloane just wasn't interested, and knowing that for sure might actually crush her more than any avalanche ever could. "Soup sounds good."

Chapter 20

Bev threw open the door as soon as they were close. "You two look like messes. Are you alright?"

"We're alright," Sloane nodded, giving her a hug. "Cold, but alright."

"If you came to help, I'm not letting you."

"You can't do all this yourself."

"Sure I can," Bev said, closing the door behind them. "I'm already half done. There aren't that many of them, I'm perfectly capable of handling it on my own." She returned to the stove, stirring a huge pot and adding ten twists of the black pepper grinder. "You need soup."

"Yes, please," Max said, sitting at the counter. "I feel like I'm frozen from the inside out."

"You look like you tangled with a bear," Bev said, almost laughing. "What happened to your clothes?"

"Thorns," Max said, and left it at that.

"Lots of thorns," Sloane added, catching Max's eye and trying not to laugh. "The trails need some serious maintenance."

Bev slid two full bowls of chili across the counter. "I almost can't believe you found him. Where was he?"

"Near the northern trail head. I think he got lost, turned around near that cliff-edge. He was about two hundred feet off the path, but already unconscious when I found him."

"Fool. You'd think that man would know better."

"Most people think they do, but don't," Max added, blowing on a spoon full of soup. "He should be just fine, they'll take care of him at the hospital."

"He'd be six feet under if it weren't for you two."

Sloane closed her eyes, relishing the soft warmth of the chili as it slid down her throat, defrosting her from the inside out. "This is delicious."

"Here, I know it's your favorite," Bev replied, setting down two huge mugs. "Mocha. You need it, after all that."

"Why are you being so nice?" Max asked. "Usually I can't get three words out of you."

"First, because Sloane is funny, and you'd know that if you spent more time listening to her and less time being hostile, and second, if I ever wind up lost in these woods, I want you two to be on my search and rescue team."

"I know she's funny," Max grumbled. "It's just usually at my expense."

"I only dish out what the other person is serving up," Sloane shot back, almost too tired to argue. "It doesn't matter. We found him, he's going to be alright."

Bev sucked her teeth, looking at both of them in turn. "Are you two warm enough?"

"Thawing out," Max answered. "But I need a hot shower."

"You go ahead," Sloane said, examining her face. She was already looking peaky. "I'll be alright, I'm used to this. More than you, anyway."

"Spend much time in the frosty woods, Sloane?" Bev asked.

Sloane was still looking at Max. "Now and then." She tore her gaze away, returning to her soup, the tendrils of steam rising into the air and dissipating like the adrenaline in her veins. There one moment, and gone the next. "How is the power situation looking?"

"Dismal," Bev replied, groaning. "I've got a generator here, but it won't last forever. The main hall and the lodge have generators, but the same problem." She grimaced, giving Sloane an apologetic look. "There were a couple of spares for the cabins, but the ones in the development team snagged them earlier."

"Figures," Max said, draining her bowl. "I wouldn't expect anything else from anyone who works for Syndicorp's head office."

"I brought some extra blankets from home for the two of you. I'd offer my couch, but it's already occupied by my kid's friend who got stranded out here.

All flights have been grounded until further notice, the ice is too much to deal with all at once."

Sloane scraped the last bits of chowder from her bowl, standing to rinse it in the sink. "I'm sure we'll be alright, Bev," she said, taking Max's bowl to rinse as well. "Any word from Mr. Parker?"

Bev shook her head. "Not a word. Orren has probably left at least a dozen messages between voicemail and texting. I'm betting his power is out, too, and his phone is probably dead."

"He'll have a lot to catch up on, when he finally resurfaces," Max said, stretching her arms over her head. The movement pulled at her undershirt and her parka, exposing a tiny sliver of skin. Sloane flushed and turned away to hide her face, but not before Bev saw her and raised an eyebrow.

"You betcha he will," Bev said, nodding. "If I were you, I'd grab that shower before anything else happens. We have gas, but who knows for how long?"

"I hear you, I'm going," Max said, standing up. "Can I take this?" She held a full jug of orange juice aloft with a hopeful grin.

"Take whatever you want, I think you've earned it with the day you two have had." Bev glanced at Sloane, a mischievous smile playing at the corners of her lips. "Are you going to go shower too?"

Sloane glared at her, willing her to stop talking. "I will, when Max is done. There's only one shower in the cabin."

"I'm aware."

"I'll only be about twenty minutes," Max announced, staring at the wall behind Bev. "I'm not one for long showers or anything."

"Yeah, sure, I'll see you in there," Sloane said, too quickly, and she squeezed her eyes shut, chastising herself for somehow managing to sound too eager and too nonchalant at the same time.

Max left, the door slamming closed behind her, and then Sloane finally exhaled.

"I knew there was something going on between you two," Bev whispered with a quiet cackle. "I knew it."

"There's nothing going on."

"Please, you looked like you were about to jump off the mountain just then.

What happened?"

"Nothing happened!"

Bev tossed a banana at her. "Liar."

"It doesn't matter, because we're still going to wind up being many states apart in distance. Mr. Parker will sell this place, I'll probably wind up back in Aspen, Max will..." Sloane trailed off with a groan. "Why can't things be easier?"

"You're overthinking."

"No, I'm not."

"You are, and given what I've learned about you over the past few weeks is that you'd get a gold medal if overthinking was a national sport." Bev shrugged. "There's obviously something there."

"If there was, I already screwed it all up."

"I don't know about that."

Sloane sighed, setting the banana on the counter. "I do. Besides, it's not meant to be, not with how things are going. Not with how everything is just..." she trailed off, waving her arm in the air with a vague gesture. "You know."

"I don't know, care to explain it to me?"

"Not really."

"You're really going to let her go because of some misunderstanding?" Bev asked. "I thought you'd have more guts than that."

"It's not a misunderstanding, it's everything else. It's this place getting sold off, it's me going back to Aspen, it's—"

"Do you want to go back to Aspen?"

"Of course."

Bev arched an eyebrow. "Really?"

"What else am I going to do, if not that?"

"Whatever you want."

Sloane pressed her palms against the counter, almost savoring the slight pain as the scarlet tiles bit into her hand. "And can you even imagine what my parents would say? I drop out of qualifiers, get a seasonal job halfway across the country, and then, what, just never go home again?"

"Would that really be so bad?"

"Yes!" Sloane shot back, before adding, "I don't know. Maybe. No."

Bev cracked two eggs at once into a bowl, whisking them smooth. "You're at a crossroads, and only you can decide what's next."

"I don't know if I'm qualified to make that decision."

"None of us are qualified to run our own lives, but here we are anyway, messing up, making mistakes, turning down the wrong road. At the end of it all, I don't want my regrets to outweigh everything else." Bev shrugged and dredged a chunk of meat through the egg before plopping it with a wet slap into a bowl of breadcrumbs. "Get out of my kitchen, Sloane."

"What?"

"Get. Out. Of my kitchen."

"Why?"

"Because I said so, for one, and for another, you're not going to get any closer to making a decision in here."

"Alright, fine, I'm going." Sloane tossed the banana back, and Bev caught it in one hand. "She's probably done with the shower now, anyway."

"I'll leave food for you in the main hall, okay?"

"Yeah, thanks Bev." Sloane hesitated a moment. "For everything." She pulled the door shut behind her, slowly heading back to the cabin, her limbs heavy, but not just from the out of cycle shift. There was a reluctance in her, something that didn't want to let go of what she'd imagined for herself. In a strange way, it was almost like grieving. She pushed the door open slowly, barely peering inside.

"Hurry up, Hearst, the heating is out and you're letting out all the warmth."

"Sorry," Sloane said, latching it behind her. She stood on the mat inside, unmoving.

"Shower is still hot, but I don't know for how long with all these developers or whatever in the other cabins."

"Thanks."

"You did good today."

Sloane glanced at her and stepped off the mat, removing her boots and parka. "We both did."

"I wasn't able to shift when I needed to."

"You did in the end, though."

"Yeah, because I thought I was going to get eaten by a polar bear."

"In Michigan?"

Max laughed, bending over to rub a towel over her short hair. "Stranger things have happened, you know."

"At least there are no poachers."

"You're right about that." Outside, a small group of the Syndicorp team bumbled past, arguing about the lack of electricity. Max's eyes followed them until they were out of sight. "I'd shower now, before those jokers take what's left of the hot water."

"Yeah, I guess I'd better." Sloane bent, taking clean clothes from her bag. Shirt, thermals, socks, underwear. "How are you feeling?" She pulled her braid out, loosening each section until it fell loose around her shoulders.

"Rough, but nothing more food won't fix. I've worked worse jobs with worse ailments, I'll survive."

"Don't ignore it, or you'll wind up feeling even more terrible than you already do." Sloane paused in the doorway of the bathroom before latching it closed. "Last time, I was sick for three days."

"That's not so bad."

"I mean it, you'll feel terrible."

"Maybe I was born to shift off-cycle, you don't know."

Sloane snorted a laugh. "I can literally hear how tired you are."

"Not so tired, just mildly fatigued."

"We'll see about that."

"So when was your first time?" Max asked, quieter now, her voice muffled through the door. "To shift, I mean."

"I was thirteen. My mom threw a party, everyone said my future was all set for me, decided, I'd go into skiing and carry on that leg of the family tradition." Sloane turned on the hot water, stepping beneath the stream and letting it wash over her, carrying away the dirt and grit that had settled on her skin after she'd shifted back. "What about you?"

"I was eleven. My family accepted it, in that way that they accept it enough to let you hang around, but they don't want to be reminded of what you are."

"Ah." Sloane scrubbed shampoo into her scalp, grateful for the feeling of it. "I know that story, just not with being a Bear."

"In this day and age? What are they, relics of the past?"

"In a sense."

"What do they expect, then, that you'd marry someone you hated just for the aesthetic?"

Sloane laughed, nearly inhaling water from the shower. "That's exactly what they expect, because it's exactly what they all did."

"Is having a deeper bank account really worth it for them?"

"Yes."

"Really?" Max asked, and the wood of the bunk creaked softly as she sat back on the thin mattress. "What a miserable existence."

"It's not one I wanted for myself. I..." Sloane trailed off, trying to gather her thoughts but failing. In an instant, the water turned from nicely heated to ice cold, like an icicle drilling down into her spine. She gave a little screech and jumped out of the stream, trying to rinse the suds from her hair without it touching the rest of her.

"What's the matter?"

"Hot water's out."

"I told you they'd take the rest of it."

"I never doubted you." Sloane turned off the water, wrapping herself in a towel, already shivering. "I hope the power comes back soon, we won't be able to open the slopes without it."

"I love that that's your biggest concern right now."

"What should it be?"

"Not freezing to death tonight."

"I guess in the worst case scenario, we can sleep in the lobby of the main hall. There would be the added bonus of making the investors uncomfortable." Sloane dressed quickly, her hair wrapped in a towel, rubbing her arms vigorously to generate heat from friction.

"After what Bev said about the reserves, I bet they limit the generators to just the lodge rooms tonight."

Sloane pushed the door open and reached for her hair dryer before she stopped, her hand hovering over it. "Oh."

"That won't work without power, Hearst."

"No, I realize that, I just wasn't thinking." She braided her hair quickly, desperate to get it off of her, the cold wetness seeping through her top already. "I probably shouldn't have washed my hair."

"After dragging Lyons through the woods? I'd say it was probably necessary."

"Yeah it's just—it's cold," Sloane said, laughing. The room was dark, and her phone was already almost dead from using it as a flashlight in the bathroom. "It's fine." She climbed into the top bunk, pulling the blankets over herself, shivering nonetheless. "So what do you think will happen now?" she asked.

"Hearst, your shivering is shaking the entire bed."

"Sorry."

Max shifted on the bottom bunk, the blankets making a quiet rasp as they dragged against each other. "Are you going to be okay?"

"Yeah, sure. Just cold. The off-season shift probably isn't helping."

"Did you have some juice?"

"Sure," Sloane answered. "That only helps so much when it's this cold."

"I bet the slopes are going to be fantastic tomorrow."

"Yeah." A strange, quiet moment passed, and there was an odd tension that settled over the room, the feeling of the few seconds before she tipped over the edge of a mountain, or a shooting star across a moonless night sky, or unwritten words yet to be solidified. Something like potential, indeterminately mixed with the trepidation of knowing that one wrong move would disturb the fragile, glassy surface of the makings of magic, sending ripples to disrupt what might have been.

"You're still shivering," Max said.

"I'm still cold."

"You could—you could sleep down here, if you wanted. It might be warmer. Probably would be warmer, I run hot."

"Okay." Sloane didn't know what else to say, and didn't want to say no, so she climbed down from the top bunk and stood at the foot of the bed, staring, blankets in hand.

"Come on, then," Max whispered, making room. "We can't have you freezing to death overnight. They'll want photographs in the morning, you know."

"I don't know about that."

"Please, a renowned skier drags some guy out of the woods, half-frozen, during a blizzard? It's the feel-good story everyone wants this time of year. Good will to your fellow humans or whatever."

Sloane crawled onto the bed, shimmying beneath the covers, clinging to the edge to take up as little space as possible. She didn't want to impose, even though she'd been invited. "I guess," she replied.

"You don't have to sleep on the edge, you know."

"It's a small bed, I don't want to keep you from sleeping."

Max pulled the blankets to one side, nodding at the empty space in front of her. "You won't."

"Are you sure?"

"I wouldn't have offered if I wasn't sure."

Sloane adjusted her weight, moving closer to the center of the bed. The back of her thigh connected with Max's hand, and she swallowed back a small gasp at the sizzle of contact, but didn't move. "Thank you," she whispered.

"Better?"

"Much."

"Good." Max moved closer, resting her arm on her own hip, but hesitating, her gestures stilted and delayed. "You'll get warmer faster if I put my arm around you."

"Is this a ploy, Maxine Carter?" Sloane asked it in what she hoped was a joking, teasing tone, but when the words crossed her lips, they sounded almost desperate.

"Would that be such a bad thing?"

"No." Sloane grabbed her hand, pulling it across her stomach. "You're right, that is warmer."

"How cold are you?"

"Extremely cold. Borderline hypothermic, in fact, I'm pretty sure I might get frostbite if you're not careful."

Max laughed into Sloane's wet hair, her breath ghosting across Sloane's neck. It drew goosebumps across her collarbone and down her arms, and there was no stopping it. "Now who's got ploys?" Max asked, and then went quiet for a long, undisturbed moment. "Am I misreading this?"

Without a word, words being superfluous then, unnecessary against the cliff-edge of yearning, of never having wanted anything more in the world, not nationals, not acceptance, not magazine covers or the newest skis, but Max Carter pressed up against her in bed, breathing across her neck, mumbling questions into her shoulder. Sloane pressed herself back into Max, pulling her arm closer, negating any distance left between them.

Turning, Sloane caught Max's stare, her eyes glinting in the almost moonless night like a forbidden sparkle, hand blown glass beads, or the way a lake glints in the summer just before the splash as skin meets water. She pressed her lips to Max's, soft and slow, like the way a perfectly ripe berry should be eaten.

"Oh," Max said softly.

Sloane kissed her again, but this time it was fiery, the omnipresent spice of a late season chili, burning gently across their lips, pressing further, harder, and sliding her tongue into Max's mouth was the sweetest sensation she'd ever had the dangerous pleasure of experiencing. She might drown in it, she might never come up for air, she might be happy to slowly rot at the bottom of the ocean for just one more kiss in that cabin.

She wasn't cold anymore. Heat spread through her body in flashes, radiating out from every place Max brushed against her with wanting fingertips. Thigh, stomach, shoulder, sternum, pushing up thick, insulated fabric to get at the soft flesh underneath like it was all she needed to survive a long winter, and maybe it was.

The cabin was quiet, with no sounds other than the quiet moans into open mouths and the snap of elastic against hip as Sloane's fingers tugged at the waistband of Max's boxers, questioning at first, and then fervent when Max returned the gesture. Sloane tossed them to the ground, staying beneath the covers where it wasn't just warm but almost stifling in a way she couldn't get enough of. She kissed down Max's collarbones, resting her lips for a moment between two small breasts as her hands kneaded gently before dipping down to hips and thighs, opening Max's legs like something precious, an early spring flower, delicate and intrepid.

"Don't make me *wait*, Sloane," Max uttered in a voice husky and needy.

She was right, and Sloane didn't want to wait anymore, either. It was like her whole life had been leading up to that, to the quiet moan that whispered past Max's lips as she teased, pressing, exploring, waiting for the right moment. Max lifted her hips off the bed, doing the work of it for her, bearing down against her palm.

Sloane adjusted her position, straddling Max's thigh, pushing down against her and already nearing the knife-edge of the precipice, trying to fight it back down, but there was no stopping it once it started. She bent, kissing Max again, muffling their greedy cries against the quiet night with tongue and heavy gasps of air until they'd both tumbled over the cliff twice, and Max pulled weakly at her arm.

"Come here," Max said, dragging her back down onto the bed.

"I'm not cold anymore, at least."

"Yeah, I'd hope not, after that."

Sloane kissed her again, her lips almost bruised from it. "Can I stay here? I wouldn't want to start shivering again."

"I think we might have to do that a few more times tonight in order to keep you warm." Max glanced at the flurry of clothing, strewn across the room. "Might as well not bother with any of that, then."

"I'm sorry I pulled away in the woods," Sloane said, turning to face the wall but pulling Max's arm tight around herself, savoring the slight friction of skin on skin.

"I understand why you did."

"I never wanted to hurt you."

Max laughed, quiet and throaty. "Stop apologizing, Hearst. We're alright."

Chapter 21

True to her expectations and the fact that the snow plows had worked through the night, there were already two reporters waiting outside the main hall when Max emerged from the cabin, leaving Sloane sleeping in the bed, tucked under the pile of blankets.

"Can I help you?" she asked brightly, already wanting them to go away. They were shattering the moment that she'd wished would last forever, but they were there nonetheless, hungry for the story that would drag Sloane back to Aspen and dump Crimson Oak into the hands of Syndicorp.

"We're looking for Sloane Hearst," a slender man improperly dressed for the weather said, holding out a small recording device. "We got word she dragged the editor of Winter Sports Magazine from the woods yesterday, saving his life."

"Oh? And where did you hear that from?"

"From Mr. Lyons himself."

"Ah." Max glanced past the building to the parking lot, spying three more cars than usual. "I trust he's been discharged from the hospital, then."

"Fit as a fiddle."

"Have you checked in with reception yet?"

"We were told to wait."

Max offered him a grin that was more of a flash of teeth than anything else. "I guess you'll have to continue to wait, then." She pushed past the reporters to get to reception, taking the back door inside and locking it behind her. "Orren?" she called.

"It's about to be a damned circus here," he replied, poking his head around the corner. He handed her a cup of coffee, and she took it gratefully. "Reporters already showing up, no sign of Mr. Parker yet, and the power came back on early this morning, so we're going to be rammed in about ninety minutes." He tilted his head. "Where's Sloane?"

"Sleeping."

"Still?"

"Yesterday was a lot, Orren." Max sipped at the coffee, raising an eyebrow in surprise. "You put sugar in this."

"I thought you deserved it, after yesterday's activities."

"One whole sugar cube, I'm like a horse that's behaved well on a trail ride."

"Carter—"

She waved him away. "Relax, I'm joking. Thank you for the coffee. I have a feeling we're going to need it."

"I told them we'll have a press conference at noon."

Max checked her watch and grimaced. "That's only a couple of hours away."

"It's not my fault you decided to sleep in the morning after the biggest blizzard this county has seen in over thirty years."

"Pardon me, I used up all my energy stomping through the forest looking for a fool who got himself lost."

"That's another thing."

"What's another thing?"

Orren leaned back against his desk, slurping noisily at his coffee. "Mr. Lyons wants to meet you and Sloane in the main hall as soon as you're both ready."

"What? Why?"

"To thank you for saving his life, if I had to wager a guess."

"The press seemed to have the idea that it was only Sloane who participated in that little venture."

"One I tried to disabuse them of, but you know how it is." He swirled the remnants of the coffee in his cup and shrugged. "He got back on site a few hours ago, and the reporters showed up not long after."

"Figures. I bet it will be some nice headlines for his fancy magazine."

"He's already waiting in the main hall." Orren gave her a pointed look and a sigh in the form of an elongated clearing of his throat.

"Alright, I hear you. I'll go get her." As she turned to open the back door, there was a knock on it.

"Good morning," Sloane said, leaning forward before glancing past her and spotting Orren. "Morning," she called to him.

"You're needed in the main hall. Mr. Lyons wants to extend his personal thanks."

"I—that's not really necessary."

"I'm not sure you'll get out of this one, Ms. Hearst. Two reporters have already arrived. I told them we'd have a press conference at noon."

"Noon! But that's barely two hours from now. Where's Mr. Parker?"

Orren grimaced. "I finally got a hold of him a little while ago. He's on his way in, but he's in a tizzy, worried this press will negatively impact the sale. He's already been on the phone with some of the investors all night, to no avail. Syndicorp might be pulling out of the deal."

"What? Why?"

"They see a lack of return on investment within the timeframe they have established in their reports, apparently." Orren sighed, setting his empty mug down on the desk. "Mr. Parker is adamant that if this deal doesn't go through, he's closing mid-season."

"But we just got dumped on with snow!" Max protested. "We'll be full up tomorrow, I guarantee it."

"He says that his accountant has warned him against any ill-advised optimism."

"So we save Lyons, drag him out of the woods, and our reward is getting turfed out of our jobs and sent home?"

"Yeah." Orren turned away, bracing his palms against the smooth wood of the desk. "Merry Christmas, I guess."

"Is Lyons already in the main hall?" Sloane asked, straightening her shoulders.

Orren nodded, still facing away from them. "He's waiting for you."

"Come on, Max, let's go find out what he wants."

Max gave her a quizzical look. "What? Didn't you hear what Orren just said?”

“I did, but that doesn’t change the fact that we have to talk to him, and to the press.”

“You do, not me. They’re all under the illusion that it was you who single-handedly dragged him out of the forest.”

Sloane laid a hand on her shoulder, a light touch that somehow managed to sink through three layers of clothing and one of skin, resting deep in her bones. “Come with me.”

“Alright, fine.”

“The press conference will be on the stairs in the main hall, so don’t go far after this display of gratitude,” Orren said. “Go on, go.”

“What about you?” Max asked.

“I’ll be fine,” he answered sadly. “Nothing can last forever.”

Sloane tugged at her sleeve, and Max nodded, reaching for the back door. “Come on, let’s go the back way, or those reporters are going to accost you.”

The morning was bright and crisp as they emerged from reception, the sweet scent of pine lilting on the breeze, wafting through the air and curling around them like delicate tendrils. “Good morning,” Sloane said again, reaching down to squeeze Max’s hand.

“Don’t.”

“Don’t?”

“You heard Orren, this place is finished. You’re going back to Aspen, I’m headed back home. Let’s not make this any more complicated than it has to be.”

“You’re underestimating the power of the season,” Sloane said. “I have a feeling everything is going to work out just fine.”

“Why, are you buying this place?”

“I wish. My parents might have money, but I only have what I’ve gotten from sponsorships. Definitely not enough to buy this place off of Mr. Parker.”

Max paused, her hand on the brass door knob. “What do we do if he knows we shifted? If he asks?”

“Lie, obviously.”

“What if he doesn’t believe us?”

"He will." Sloane pulled the other side open, sauntering through with an odd air of confidence Max hadn't seen before. It had an authenticity that was new, and it was bright like a magnesium spark, like she couldn't look at her without having to blink away the potential.

"If you say so."

Mr. Lyons, now significantly pinker and less frozen, was sitting at a table in the conference room, which was awash with at least a dozen different gift baskets. He tugged at the thick knitted scarf that hung loose around his neck and tugged at the zip on his parka. "Ladies, it is an honor to make your acquaintance." He nodded to Sloane. "You've been on my cover. I'm sorry I haven't made your acquaintance before." He stayed seated, gesturing to the chairs across from him. "I will remain sitting, I hope that's not too rude, but I was advised to take it easy for a few days."

Sloane sat across from him, folding her hands in her lap. "I hope you are feeling better."

"I'd be dead if not for you."

"Both of us. I never would have made it out of the woods in time without Max's help."

He reached across the oak table to shake Max's hand. "Ms. Carter, I presume. I can only offer my thanks, and what is probably an overabundance of gift baskets. My husband said it may have been a little overboard."

Max cracked a smile. "I'm sure it will all get eaten."

"Ms. Hearst, I wanted to know what you'd decided about Syndicorp's offer about the corporate job in Aspen."

"What?" Max asked, jerking away from the table. "You didn't tell me about that."

Sloane shot her a look and then turned to smile at Lyons. "I'd decided not to take them up on their offer."

"Because you didn't like the work, or because you don't like Aspen?"

"In honesty, Mr. Lyons, both. My strengths do not lie in business administration."

"You're a strong pull for any lodge or resort." He gestured towards the decorations that hung from the banisters. "This place could really be something with just a few adjustments."

"Then you want Orren Ralt and Max Carter at the helm," Sloane answered, sitting back in her chair. "They are unparalleled. They know this place better than Parker does. Without Max and Orren, I'm not so sure we'd be sitting here amid piles of aged cheese and wine in wicker baskets."

Mr. Lyon's' gaze flicked from Sloane to Max, and he raised an eyebrow. "I'm sure you've heard that Syndicorp pulled the deal."

"We did hear something to that effect."

"Then why tell me this?" he asked.

Max leaned forward, folding her hands on the table. "You want Sloane for the job, just not with Syndicorp."

Lyons drummed his fingers against the polished wood. "I'd be lying if I said the thought hadn't crossed my mind as I was laying in that hospital bed."

"What about your position as an investor?" Sloane asked. "Syndicorp won't be happy if you undermine them."

"They already pulled the deal, they're dragging their management back to Aspen on the first flight they can make. Besides, I'm not beholden to them, I barely wanted to be on their committee in the first place. A favor to my father, you see." He glanced at Sloane. "Something I'm sure you'd be more than familiar with."

"Unfortunately," Sloane agreed.

"I went into the woods yesterday a curious man. There's something different about this mountain that I can't quite put my finger on, but I just had to see more of it."

"It's different from other places," Max said. "It feels different because it is different. Mr. Lyons, this place has incredible potential."

"Convince me, Ms. Carter."

"Programs, year-round." Max stood, pointing out the window at the slopes. "More instructors, community programs, grants to cover costs for schools and weekend packages for teens. We could get a ski jump in over there, on the west face of the mountain. I've always thought it was perfect for that, and it would attract people like Sloane here to come train at the lodge."

He nodded, a smile dragging at the corners of his mouth. "Go on."

"In late spring and summer, ecological programs. Grants for research in the woods, there are rare species of mushrooms in there if you know where to look, I learned from a park ranger down south. Also—" Max moved to another window, pointing out into the woods. "There's a clearing out there that would be perfect for an astronomical observatory. A small one, to be sure, but perfect for small groups." She looked at Sloane, who was staring at her with glitter in her eyes, nodding at her. "Sloane Hearst could start building that program, she has a strong base knowledge of the stars. That is, if she wanted to stay here at Crimson Oak."

"I would stay," Sloane replied quietly.

"What about nationals?" Lyons asked.

"I don't know about nationals, but I can say that I'm a good teacher, and will continue to be, if you had room for me here." Sloane tore her stare from Max and looked back to him. "Mr. Lyons, you should see Max snowboard. She's one of the best I've ever seen, but she needs sponsors. If you want this place to have name recognition, you'd do well to invest in her."

Lyons tapped a rhythm into the arms of his chair, considering. "I think we could work something out."

"Sir, you don't have to do that just because we—"

"A near death experience tends to change a man," he interrupted. "I want to spend my time in a place like this."

Sloane cleared her throat. "Parker said he'd close this week if the deal fell through. We'd both be sent back, which would be a shame, because there's so much we could begin planning here, if you were serious."

"Don't worry about that, my lawyer is already drawing up paperwork."

"And we'd want decent contracts," Max said. "Full time, year-round."

He nodded. "Of course."

"Housing on-site for the other contractors."

"We'll move back to on-site staff, I think. Better employee retention, which will be important in a place like this."

Max leaned against the door frame, pushing her hair back. "Is this really happening?"

"On one condition," Lyons said.

"What's that?" Sloane asked.

"We announce the acquisition at the press conference."

* * *

"Hello, and welcome to Crimson Oak," Mr. Parker said, fumbling with the note cards in his hands. It was obvious from the shaking in his voice that he wasn't a fan of public speaking. "I know several of you are here because of what happened yesterday, and so I will hand the floor over to Walter Lyons before we discuss anything further."

Lyons stood, bracing himself against the banister at the foot of the grand staircase. "Isn't this a beautiful place?" he asked, and it was rhetorical. "A stunning, beautiful slice of landscape, and that's why I made the very foolish decision to go for a walk in the woods during a blizzard. You'd think someone like me would know better. Clearly, I did not."

The crowd of ten or fifteen reporters tittered, but settled after a quick moment.

"Predictably, I got lost. Lucky for me, these two women made it their mission to find me, and they saved my life. I can never repay them for that kindness."

"Sir," the lean reporter said, stepping forward. "Sir, our reports said that Sloane Hearst, professional skier, saved you."

"We both did," Sloane said, standing at the top of the stairs. "I couldn't have done what I did without the help of Max Carter, professional snowboarder."

"Ms. Hearst, what about national qualifiers?"

"I don't think I need nationals," she said simply. "I've found something else that suits me better."

The reporters murmured with concern, and Max stepped forward, her head tilted upwards in defiance. "This press conference isn't about Ms. Hearst's career, it's about how Mr. Lyons survived a blizzard on a mountain with challenging terrain. Had he not been a skilled outdoorsman, he wouldn't be standing in front of you today."

"Ms. Carter, how did you decide to go looking for him?" another reporter asked.

"It's what anyone would have done in the same situation. It was teamwork between me, Sloane Hearst, and Orren Ralt, who organized the emergency services response once we located him."

Mr. Parker cleared his throat, sifting through his note cards. "I'd also like to announce that Crimson Oak is going to be entering a new phase of development under the direction and ownership of Lyons' Pride Lodging. The deal will be finalized before the end of the year."

"Where will you go now?" a reporter asked.

"I'm retiring to California," Parker said. "I've had enough snow, I want sun and beaches now." He tried for a smile, eventually finding it. "Maybe I'll take up surfing."

"Hey," Sloane whispered, pulling Max to the side of the banister. The reporters were in a flurry, all asking questions about the deal now that they knew Lyons was moving into winter sports lodge investment. "You did amazing."

"I couldn't have done it without you."

"We make a good team."

Max slipped an arm around her waist, ignoring the flash of the cameras below. "Yeah, I mean, I hope you realize that you're going to have to do all the decorating now. There's no way Orren or I could even do half as much as this." She swallowed hard, her eyes meeting Sloane's. "I don't want you to leave."

"Then maybe I don't have to." Sloane laughed, and then glanced up. "Forgot I put that there."

"Mistletoe? Really?"

"Just go with it, Carter."

"You don't have to tell me twice." Max twisted her fingers into Sloane's hair, pulling her in, a hand on her back and dipping her back into a kiss. The cameras flashed, and pencils scribbled, but it didn't matter.

They'd both gotten exactly what they needed, and the future spread out in front of them, unknown but sparkling with possibility.

CHAPTER 21

* * *

About the Author

A huge thanks to my most tireless supporter, my wife, who told me to write this book, and came up with the name. You were all saved from far inferior titles thanks to her efforts.

Thank you to my readers, who are the reason I get up in the morning, make coffee, and sit down to write. Without you, I'd probably descend into jazz and liquor. Your support means that I keep writing, and for that, I thank you from the bottom of my icy, snow-filled heart.

You can connect with me on:
- https://ryannfletcher.com
- https://twitter.com/IMRyannFletcher
- https://facebook.com/RyannFletcherWrites
- https://instagram.com/RyannFletcherWrites
- https://www.tiktok.com/@ryannfletcherwrites

Subscribe to my newsletter:
- http://eepurl.com/gOQBaP

Also by Ryann Fletcher

Deus Ex Mechanic

Alice is the best mechanic the corrupt Coalition regime has ever seen. When she's kidnapped by an infamous vigilante space pirate named Violet, she has to make the hardest decision she's ever made: escape back to the comfort of the Coalition, or risk everything to fight injustice?

When Violet decided to ransack Coalition vessels, she never though she'd have to fight her feelings for Alice, too. Will giving into an affair with the treasonous mechanic cloud her judgment and jeopardize the safety of her crew? As they fight side by side against ruthless rival pirate captain Leo and his crew, will they grow closer together, or will everything fall apart and leave them stranded in dark space?